DIYHEARTS
A #LOVEHACK STORY

Verlene Landon

COPYRIGHT

DIY Hearts
a #LoveHack story
Verlene Landon
Copyright © 2019 Verlene Landon - Rusty Halo Books
All rights reserved.

Editing: Missy Borucki
Cover Design: Amy at Q Design
Cover Photo: Wander Aguiar
Cover Model: Barrett S.
Proofing: Angela Campbell

ISBN: 978-0998126760

DEDICATION

To Apothic Wines and Lee's Liquor, without you, this book would have never happened.

VERONICA

"**W**ait! I'm sorry, this is your home too, and I have no right to tell you not to have a guest."

Jess's shoulders dropped and she turned to face Ronny. Her body and face had relaxed but she was clearly at the end of her rope. Ronny wanted to scream, *Please, don't give up on me! I'll get better, I promise,* but she knew it for the lie it was.

She was damaged beyond repair and she'd lashed out at the one person who cared. There was no getting better, or "fixing" her, no matter how hard Jessica tried. Ronny was ruining her best friend's life with her inability to move forward and let go of the past.

Jess hugged her and she froze. After a few moments she regained her composure and returned the embrace but not as eagerly as she'd hoped. *Heck, if I can't even hug my best friend without cringing what hope do I have for a normal life or a relationship . . . or children.*

Jess ended the embrace and gazed up at her with pity in her soft brown eyes. It was a look Ronny hated. Who wanted to be pitied?

Not for the first time, she looked down at her friend wishing she were more like her. Ronny thought Jessica was beautiful with her brown eyes and hair, average height and weight. Being average wasn't an insult and it helped Jessica blend-in.

Unlike Ronny. She stood out like a sore thumb no matter what.

Not only was she freakishly tall, measuring a bit over five foot eleven, she was a natural red head, and her eyes were unusual too. Almost violet in color, her mother called them Elizabeth Taylor eyes.

Her differences had always been something she'd played up. Wearing purple eyeliner and clothes to make her eyes pop. Donning heels to look even taller and keeping her hair natural.

She used to relish the attention being so unusual brought her, but now? Now she wore brown contacts when she went out, if she went out in public at all. She dyed her hair but the color washed out within a week. Plus, she wore baggy clothes and walked hunched in on herself. *Yet more things stolen from me.*

Maybe if I hadn't dressed that way, I wouldn't be in this mental mess today?

Ronny knew these questions only spiraled her down to the depths of despair and shame. The logical part of her knew it wasn't her fault, but sometimes she couldn't seem to hold on to that truth.

Unbidden, tears sprang to her eyes. *When would she stop feeling him on top of her, inside her? When would his words go silent? "Do you know how many times I came in and watched you at night? How much self-control I showed by not taking you any of those times?"*

"Hey, now. Don't cry. I can read up on leaky pipes and probably fix it myself. No worries," said Jess.

Ronny knew the pipe repair was only half of it. Jessica wanted to get Clayton over here so she could rekindle an old flame that was extinguished prematurely. He was all she'd talked about since running into him three days ago at Food Bear.

Jessica didn't think Ronny knew she drove into the next county when she went out hoping to run into him accidently. *Next county out here is only twenty miles but still.*

All those trips were in vain because Clay had literally moved not ten miles from Gram's house. *Well, my house now.* God, how she wished she'd moved here two years ago right after her grandmother passed. For a hot minute, she had entertained the idea, but quickly discarded it in favor of the hustle and bustle of city life.

Taking a deep breath, Ronny knew she had to do this for her friend. Jess had done so much for her and she couldn't pay her back by not allowing other people in the house they shared. Other than her trips to "accidently" run into Clayton, Jess did practically nothing for herself.

"Call Clayton, ask him to come fix the pipe. I'll be fine. I'll just stick to my room with headphones on and you can call me when it's over."

"Are you sure, Ron? I don't want to set you back."

"It's been three hundred and twelve days and I haven't really gotten far enough to have a *setback*. A setback would indicate progress, which I haven't exactly excelled at. Backward at this point would be in that apartment..."

She couldn't even bear to repeat what had happened. She'd seen numerous counselors and none of them could give her back her power or independence. Her sense of self-worth didn't exist anymore.

None of them could help her accept how she'd given up to the point that when he'd died of a heart attack—hours into her assault—she'd just lain there, unmoving. Barely breathing. It wasn't until Jessica called her about missing their coffee meet-up that she'd snapped out of the trance.

It was like he'd stolen all her accomplishments, both past and future when he took her body without her permission. She was a useless husk of what was once a vibrant woman with a talent for design and a zest for life.

4

Veronica Beth Allen was nothing more than a ghost. A ghost who haunted her late grandmother's country home and dampened her best friend's love life.

"Only if you're absolutely positive. You mean more to me than anyone and I don't want to cause you pain."

"The only way you'll cause me pain is if you keep putting your life on hold for me. Besides he's the only thing you've talked about, so, yes, I'm positive."

Ronny was *not* positive, but she knew that Jess had been crushing on Clay for a long time. They went on one date in college but decided to just be friends. That didn't extinguish the torch Jess carried for him though.

After Jess ran into Clay three days ago, she finally added a detail that made some things click into place. She'd loaned him money to start a construction business. He'd paid her back with interest in less than two years, but Ronny got the distinct impression that Jessica felt like that should count for something. Like maybe he owed her. It was the one thing about her friend she didn't like. No human being owed another in any emotional or physical way . . . ever.

My landlord said I owed him for teasing and for wearing certain clothes.

Stop it.

Ronny was almost positive there were no deep feelings involved between the two of them. But he still mattered to Jess for whatever reason, so she would put her needs aside for once.

"You're the best, Ronny. I won't ever let anyone I invite into your home hurt you. You know what this proves to me?" She could do nothing more than shake her head. It didn't prove anything other than what a basket case she was.

"It proves to me that you *are* getting better. You aren't beyond repair, as you seem to insist. The Ronny I know is stronger than she thinks." Another quick hug and Ronny was extended beyond her tolerance for the day.

"I'm going to go call Clay now." A giddy Jessica danced down the hall. Seeing her friend happy almost made it worthwhile to know there would be a man in the house and them at his mercy . . . almost.

CLAYTON

When Clay pulled up to the address Jessica had given him, there was a slight hint of familiarity, but nothing he could grasp. He was slightly surprised it wasn't a sprawling country home. Jessica liked things over the top. *I guess if you have the money you can do things whatever way you want.*

Clay didn't have the same luxury as his friend, but the truth was, he *liked* things modest. Even if he had a surplus of money it would still be this cozy style country home he'd buy. He was a simple man with simple tastes. He didn't drink imported beer or drive a fancy car. He patted his twenty-year-old truck as he lifted the toolbox from the back. *Yep, it suits me just fine.*

Stepping onto the creaky but sturdy porch, he noticed a note on the door instructing him to just enter and go to the left and the bathroom with the leak would be down on the right.

There weren't any vehicles parked in the drive, but they could be in the barn he noticed to the right of the house. Jessica must have had to run out. Doing as the note instructed, he made his way down the hall and to the last door on the right. Opening it revealed not a bathroom but a bedroom. A quick scan told him it was most assuredly Jessica's room. It was decorated with red silky and satiny materials. The furniture looked like it cost more than what he paid for his entire trailer with furnishings did.

The bed linens even had a designer logo repeatedly printed on them so no one could mistake them for a sheet set from Wal-Mart.

Even with all her money and champagne taste, Jessica was a good person at heart, a little uppity when around her rich friends and family, but good people. Which was rare in his experience among the Richie Rich's of the world.

Just as he was about to step into the bathroom, the door to the sauna in the corner opened and out stepped a barely covered Jessica.

His eyes briefly skimmed the cedar planked and smoked glass box sitting catty-corner across from the entrance.

"Jesus." He stepped back bumping into the bed he'd just been eyeing and landing on his ass with a bounce.

"So eager to jump into my bed I see." Her voice was dropped low. She laughed like it was a joke, but Clay wasn't convinced. She'd made no secret from the day they met that she wanted more from him.

Jessica didn't take no for an answer so he took her out once just to show her how incompatible they would be as a couple. Clay could barely afford his used books at the time they met, and she was sprinting around campus in a brand-new sports car.

He ate Ramen for lunch while hers looked more like a three-course affair with food he'd never heard of. Clay was happy they never crossed that line because she'd meant a lot to him as a friend—even though they grew apart over the years—and they would have never had that had he given in.

Plus, Clay was convinced her fascination with him was based solely on his *no.* She wanted what she couldn't have.

To be honest, Clay found it a little intriguing, how she could act so wholly different depending on the company. When they hung out, she wore jeans and drank beer just like him, but if her rich friends or family were around, she acted more like them.

The truth was found in her eyes most of the time. It was clear to anyone who cared to notice, that while she enjoyed the finer things in life, she wasn't happy acting like a rich bitch.

Bottom line though, he owed her big time. He wouldn't be where he was today if not for her encouragement and money, so he'd do just about anything from her . . . except have sex or lead her on.

Rather than respond to her semi-joking invitation, he opted for a friendly embrace. It was awkward with her wrapped in a towel.

"Hey, Jess. How are you?"

His version of friendly and hers were not exactly the same. She let go of her towel and leaned into him, trapping the deep red terry-cloth between them. Clay waited for her to end the embrace, but she didn't. He never ended a hug first, his mom taught him that.

You never know how much the other person might need it. So, instead of pushing her away before she got the wrong idea, Clay continued to hold her.

Finally, Jessica stepped back, but when she did, her towel fluttered quickly to the floor leaving a very naked friend standing in front of him.

"Oops. Sorry, it seems I lost my towel." Her words said apology, but her twirl said it was contrived.

Clay wasn't a dead man, and he looked. Not ogled but looked before he could tell himself not to. He shouldn't have, but he did. Looking at her was a natural reaction but did nothing to turn him on. He simply didn't think of her that way and wasn't attracted to her sexually.

That didn't stop her eyes from going round and her ruby lips tipping up in a seductive smile at his momentary perusal.

More than anything he was fascinated as to how she'd been in a sauna and still had on full make-up and didn't look the least bit sweaty.

"Like what you see, sailor?"

Then it hit him, this was another one of her ploys to try to get him into her bed. Clay knew he had to be firm with her. Taking no for an answer wasn't Jessica's strong suit. He'd mucked up by looking. *Stupid, Clay, real stupid. You know how she operates.*

Clay rolled his eyes. "I don't know how many ways I can say it, you know I adore you, but we are never going to happen. We're friends, just friends, and we will always be friends, no matter what. But you've got to stop these games. Is there even a pipe leak?" Clay shook his head and turned to head out the door.

"Clay, wait. I'm sorry, but, yes, there is a leak and I need the pipe fixed. It's in there." She pointed to the right. "Let me get some clothes on and I'll show you."

She was pouty, he could tell this wasn't the end of it. Jessica saw it as a temporary setback not a firm *no*. That was a quality he appreciated in people, just not when it came to that.

Once she was dressed, she showed him the pipe and he got to work. For the most part, she left him alone.

He could hear her talking to someone—the sound echoed through pipes—someone with the voice of an angel. A broken angel if he were judging from the overwhelming notes of sadness in the voice. He couldn't make out the words, but the desolation squeezed his heart.

VERONICA

"How're you doing, Ron?" Jess had found her lying on her stomach on her bathroom floor and reading *how to for dummies* books online.

When she raised her gaze to Jess's, her friend seemed a little down. A good friend would have immediately posed the same question.

"Not as good as I want to be, but better than I expected?" Ronny hadn't meant it to come out as a question, but it did anyway.

She knew she relied way too much on her friend. Even looking to Jess confirm her own feelings rather than internalize. Somehow that seemed easier.

Maybe because it was Jess's phone call that pulled her into action that day. Shoving his lifeless body off her to grab her phone. She hid in the closet and blubbered to Jess what had happened.

She would never forget her best friend's cry of anguish as she explained. He'd been dead for God only knew how long, but she'd been terrified to move or even call the police. Jess had sprung into action and handled everything.

When the police showed up with Jess, her friend looked like a savior and she really had been. Still was.

Ronny also knew Jess couldn't babysit her forever. Her will to do so would be determined by her quality of life and well, right now, that was pretty dang low. The time was coming quicker than she cared to dwell on where she'd have to look to herself.

Jessica had been honest about applying for jobs and looking for a new place. She'd said nothing was set in stone, but Ronny figured she would be gone within a year. *I can't even blame her. She's devoted more time to me than I ever should have asked her to.*

Veronica wasn't above allowing her friend to stay as long as she was willing to, but the reality of being alone hit her over the head with a leaky pipe.

She needed to learn to do some basics around the house before Jessica left. Ronny could force herself to a home improvement store if she absolutely had to if she couldn't get a part online, but there was no way she could call a repair man into her home alone.

Shaking off her future worries she tried to be a good friend. "I guess I should ask you the same thing, how are you doing? You have frown lines right there." Ronny touched her friend's forehead before rocking her body up and placing the laptop in her lap.

Something about lounging on the cold tile of the bathroom was comforting to her. She hated her bed and never used it. Instead, she had a nest in the corner of her room she slept in.

Until she noticed Jess staring at her in utter shock, Ronny hadn't realized what she'd done. Not only was she joking, she touched her friend without asking permission.

"I'm sorry," she gasped as her hand flew to her mouth.

Jess wrapped her up so fast her head swam, but she didn't immediately cringe. "No, god no, don't apologize."

This is a moment. My first real moment. That realization was welcomed and terrifying. All her therapists swore to her she would start having moments of healing. After almost a year she'd given up hope, but she just had a moment and only a second of doubt and guilt after.

Jess had been to therapy with her a few times and she got it. Touching someone voluntarily, without asking permission, was momentous, no matter how small a touch.

"Veronica? You were drugged and nothing that happened was your fault. Why is it so important for you to grant and receive permission even for minor touches? You

said no to your attacker and he still touched you. Why is permission so extreme for you?" Dr. Davidson, her third therapist had asked while tapping her pen on her clipboard.

She hesitated to answer but Jessica sitting by her side gave her the help she needed to explain.

"Because, maybe if I'd not silently granted him permission to touch me over time, things may have been different. Every time he came to my apartment to check this or fix that, he'd brush my shoulder or move a lock of my hair. It made me uncomfortable, but I wrote it off and never said anything. Maybe—"

"Veronica, no. Nothing you did contributed to his choices. We've talked about that. Let's look forward for a bit and talk about moments. Moments that will start coming even if you can't see them now."

"Oh my god, I had a moment," she whispered reverently into her best friend's shoulder before pulling back and wrapping her arms around herself.

Watching Jess throw her hands to her mouth and her eyes start to sparkle had her bursting into tears, but not wholly sad ones.

"I'm so happy for you, Ron. Remember what Dr. Davidson said? She said once you have one, more will follow, you just have to recognize them for what they are. You'll be back to your old self in no time, who knows, maybe you'll even go on a date in this decade."

She could tell when Jess realized it was the exact wrong thing to say. Her elation at having a moment crashed and burned. Another thing Dr. D warned her about.

"Don't, Jess. It's not your fault I'm like this. So, are you going to tell me why you're frowning?" A change of subject is what she needed, and she found it.

"Clay." Jess let out a sigh and looked almost defeated. "I stood in front of the man naked and he turned me down cold. I don't know what I need to do to get his attention in that way. I know it would be so hot. Sex with him would rock my world."

Ronny worried her lip, not sure how to tell her friend that it sounded like he wasn't attracted to her and she shouldn't push it. She wanted to scold her for her tactics. To Ronny they were wrong—plain and simple. When it came to matters of consensual sex there was zero gray, only black and white. The grey was where predators exploited things.

Grey was the color of assault and date rape and *oh, I didn't know she was drunk,* or *she wanted it, she just didn't have to guts to say so.* Gray was the color of a landlord who drugged the things in her refrigerator and snuck into her apartment to masturbate. Gray was where the man raped her repeatedly and said she'd brought it on herself. *She'd wanted it, and him and just went out with others to stoke his jealously.*

Gray was a man making a woman believe it was her fault.

Black or white. Yes or no.

But instead of scolding her, Ronny said, "Well, maybe you should just move on. Find a man who appreciates you."

"Nope, I just have to up my game."

Her words struck Ronny like a blow to her chest. *Nooooooooooo*, she screamed inside, but couldn't give it voice. *You don't manipulate and trick people.*

Jessica jumped up and started dancing around like she was in a music video about single women and power. Ronny couldn't help but stare in awe at her carefree friend. She wanted that back. Of all the things she'd lost, living in the moment was top five.

Jessica stopped and pulled her phone from her pocket. "Oh, Clay's done. I should see him out."

Ronny nodded and stood. She followed her friend as far as her bedroom door before locking it and taking a deep breath.

Today had been a rough day with her emotions and her *moment.* Even so, she wasn't ready for a man to have all access to her home. Although when she heard the front door, her curiosity got the best of her and she strode over to the window. Slowly, she opened the curtain just to peek.

She needed to know what was so special about this man that had her friend dancing around and trying to seduce him after holding a torch for him for years.

The setting sun cast a long shadow across the grass before the man himself came into view. Fascinated, she watched the shadow bob and sway as he stepped down off the porch. He was backlit but she could see enough to know he wore blue jeans and flannel.

Her lips turned up just a bit at how non-threatening he seemed from behind in torn denim and what looked to be a comfy shirt.

Another moment maybe? She was looking at a man, with a tool-belt, coming from her house but wasn't in a full-blown panic. Her landlord had always worn a toolbelt and in her head she thought that would be a trigger. Since it wasn't she was counting it.

I'd say that's definitely a moment.

She watched him as he walked to the old blue Ford parked on the gravel and tossed his belt and box in the back.

After they were secured, he leaned both hands against the door and let his blond head sag between his arms, like he was replaying his day on fast-forward.

When he stood back up and shook his head, the longer hair on top fell onto his forehead. He dropped one hand to his hip, then he turned back around and stared at the house.

Ronny gasped at his startling blue eyes and razor-sharp jawline. She found herself widening the opening between the curtains to get a better look at him. He was the first man she'd looked at with anything other than disgust since she was attacked.

Clayton was beautiful for lack of a better description. She knew men weren't supposed to be called beautiful, but that's what he was.

He turned to open the driver's side door and his crystalline eyes caught hers from behind the curtain and a half smile spread across his mouth. Wide and friendly, then he threw up his hand as if to wave.

A sense of déjà vu washed over her.

Ronny didn't wave back or acknowledge him in any way, she dropped to the ground like a stone and didn't move for at least an hour. Finally, she crawled over to her nest and went to sleep.

CLAYTON

When his eyes met the angel through the window at Jess's place, he nearly lost his ability to stand. He knew beyond a shadow of a doubt that the melodic voice belonged to her.

With the way she simply vanished from his sight when he blinked, he could have easily believed her to be an actual angel. Except for the fact he'd heard Jess talking to her through the pipes.

Jessica's voice was easily recognizable with her unique cadence. It was like she was taught to over enunciate her words.

The other voice was sad, he had no other way to describe it. Sad and defeated. It gutted him even without the words. No one should sound that way. His mother had sounded that way for years.

Once he added the visual, he was struck dumb. The window she'd been looking through was immaculate, like it had just been cleaned. The setting sun glinted off the bottom corner and cast a halo of light around the figure.

The fire around her in juxtaposition to the angelic light, like heaven and hell warring for dominance. It took him a second to realize the fire was the setting sun kissing her red hair.

Her eyes were hard to make out from the distance, but he could have sworn they were a light shade.

When his wave sent her away, he almost rushed back inside to see if she'd fallen. She must have been standing on something because her head reached the top of the window.

Two things stopped him in his tracks. One, Jessica would have taken his reappearance all wrong, and two, there was a flash of terror across her face just before she disappeared.

Clay forced himself to get in his truck and leave. If the beauty had fallen, Jessica would have heard and handled it.

He wasn't sure how he knew it was terror, but somehow, he just did. So in all likelihood, she hadn't fallen, she'd left the window on purpose.

That didn't stop him from obsessing all the way to one of three things he owned outright. This one he called an office and had only bought it in the last few years since he'd paid Jessica back.

He used to have his trailer, the second thing he owned outright, on a measly acre in the next town over and ran his business from there. Now, the trailer was behind his office and would do until his house was finished.

His office was actually an old filling station with an attached garage and forty-five undeveloped acres. It worked perfectly for a construction company though. Plenty of storage space for materials and tools, plus a small office space and a place to lock up his trailers. What more could a man want?

Charlie popped his head in the door as soon as his ass hit the chair. "Hey, you're back. Old lady Wilson called, her goats got out, busted through the side of the barn again. I popped over and did a temporary patch for the night, but she wants you to handle the repair."

Of course, she does. Being a good guy sucked sometimes. Mrs. Wilson knew him since the day he was born. He'd let those old goats out enough times on purpose growing up that now she wouldn't let anyone else handle it. *It's got to be payback.*

"Thanks, Charlie, anything else happen today?" Charlie was a good guy and Clay appreciated the help. He loved being a mentor, but he had to wonder if anyone in town was ever going to trust Charlie to fix their homes.

Seeing as how Charlie didn't grow up here, Clay figured it'd take another decade, even though he was perfectly capable.

"Yeah, I went over to the tavern and handled that roof patch. Rusty was so pleased with my work, we have free drinks and wings tonight, if you're up for it."

Charlie's grin said it all. Someone in town trusted him without asking Clay to come and look it over.

Well, I'll be, miracles never cease. Now if some new construction would come in, this would be a perfect day.

"Sounds good, let me get changed. Lock up and I'll meet you out front in five."

While Charlie closed the door and whistled his way out to the garage area to lock up, Clay headed out back to his trailer. And he did so without walking around it to gaze on the progress of his soon-to-be first house. The walk-around had become his nightly routine on days he didn't find time to work on it himself. But beer and wings were calling his name.

He couldn't shake the haunted eyes and glowing hair of the mystery woman in the window so the distraction would be welcomed.

After he threw on a clean shirt and added some cologne, he headed out. Charlie waited under the awning that used to cover the old pumps.

"All locked up and ready for some wings." Charlie's nose twitched and Clay knew it was coming. "Awe, shucks, you didn't have to get all gussied up for me, but you sure do smell purdy." His accent was over the top, but at least it was all in good fun.

"This old thing, I just threw it on to cover my unmentionables." Clay's Marilyn Monroe pose gave Charlie a laugh. "But the cologne, that's all for you, darlin'."

Leave it to Charlie to wipe away the unidentified worry over the unknown woman in the window with his antics.

Clay gave him a shove. "Now, if you're done hitting on me, can we get moving? I'm starving."

The walk to The Tavern was short—across the street and down about a quarter of a mile—it wasn't really a chore, even in the humidity. However, the air conditioning that smacked him in the face when he pulled the heavy green door open was welcomed.

"Clay, Charlie, pull up a stool, I've got you covered." Rusty didn't have to tell Clay twice. By the time his backside hit the cracked green plastic, Rusty had an ice cold PBR waiting for the both of them.

"You did me good today, so enjoy. Wings'll be out in a minute. Tonight, the mugs stay full and the basket overflowing until you call uncle."

Clay appreciated it and he would have a drink or two and a basket of wings and call it even.

The perfectly poured amber liquid was irresistible considering the day Clay had. After a salute and a long drink, he returned the mug to the wooden surface.

"A mug and a basket each will do just fine. You paid for a job so no need to pay twice."

Rusty looked offended at Clay's words. "Nonsense. Any other company would have taken a week at double the price to handle that. Plus, no one else would have showed up last night during the rain and helped me move the heavy pool table out of the way to save the classic. And then mop up for me."

Turning his head to the *classic* in question. That pool table was older than Clay was. It was original to the building, even more *original* than the old man himself. If someone needed to know something about the history of Bellwood, all they had to do was ask Rusty.

He knew it all about everything and everyone. Rusty wasn't like the old church ladies wagging their tongues about it just to have something to talk about, but he knew.

Wait.

"Hey, Rusty, you know the old Jackson place? The one Jessica Robinson bought after Ms. Jackson passed? What do you know about her roommate?"

The smile that split the old man's face was a bit disturbing.

"Place ain't been sold since it was built. Still in the Jackson family."

"Oh, I guess Jessica is renting then." His voice was barely above a reflective whisper as he spoke to his beer. Clay could only assume it was a rental agent handling the estate. Dead end.

"Nope. Not a rental. Ms. Jackson, god rest, her granddaughter moved in about ten or eleven months ago. Jess came back home with her." The old man didn't elaborate, just continued cleaning the bar and wiping glasses.

Clay didn't miss his murmurs while he worked though. "Horrible business, just horrible. Sweet girl, hardly ever leaves the property."

So, the mystery woman had to be Ms. Jackson's granddaughter.

That begged the question of why Jessica was living there instead of in her own place. Her family was loaded so why she'd be living the simple life puzzled him.

"What's the deal with Jessica then?" Clay hadn't meant to pose the question aloud, hadn't even realized he had until Rusty answered.

"Family cut her off, but you didn't hear that from me."

VERONICA

Lack of sleep and caffeine made Ronny more cranky than normal. *Not that I'm not used to lack of sleep, we're old friends after all.*

While waiting for the coffee to drip she was transported in time to the reason she couldn't sleep well. So tangled up in the past, she couldn't break back into the present until she felt a burning sensation on her hand.

"Crap." Ronny hopped back and sucked the abused skin between her thumb and index finger into her mouth. When she realized what happened, she carefully removed her overflowing coffee cup from under the steady stream of brown liquid and pushed a larger one into its place.

When the cool water finally ran over her hand, she breathed a sigh of relief. She knew better than to let the past have too much power, it never ended well. However, this time it wasn't the same. Yes, she drifted back, but it happened less and less as time marched on.

What made this time different was the reason she drifted back. Lack of sleep, but not lack of sleep caused by rampant nightmares and cold sweating.

This lack of sleep was caused by the direct eye contact with Clayton. It wasn't terror that had her tossing and turning in her nest, it was the first spark of attraction she'd felt in over three hundred and twelve days.

That's what held sleep at bay. Kept the gears in her mind turning like mad, and what caused her distress.

After her burn was soothed, she sipped enough black coffee to make room for almond milk and sugar. She grabbed the other cup and did the same, sans the sipping.

Ronny took up her usual post at the breakfast table and placed the other cup to her left. On days Jess wasn't waiting for her, she joined within minutes. It was like they'd synced up over time,

Like clockwork, as she settled in to sip her brew and read what passed for news on her smart phone, Jess joined her.

Before her friend spoke, Ronny mimicked the words coming in her head. They were the same every morning and the routine was a comfort, no matter her reply.

"You're a peach, Ronny, a real peach. Heart of gold still firmly in place . . . check." Her friend sat down and blissfully tasted her coffee.

Next.

"On a scale from teenager on Elm Street to Rip Van Winkle, how did you sleep?"

When they'd first moved in together, the daily inquiry irritated her, but now the predictability was downright key to her survival.

It only took a few months of being asked before she started answering honestly.

"Teenager a block over from Elm Street, but close enough to hear one, two." The last words she sang like the movies. That was the messed-up thing about life. After all she'd suffered, she still loved horror movies, even though she had lived one.

Her therapist explained that away too. *Veronica, stop beating yourself up for surviving and coping. There is no wrong way to handle a tragedy and get back to living. Anyone who tries to tell you there is, well, they are just ignorant or a jerk . . . or both.*

When her friend's face fell and Ronny realized why, she blurted out an explanation to save her friend the sadness.

"But not for the reason you think, promise. I only had one of those moments last night and it was short lived. Got up and showered and went back to fitful sleep."

It seemed that Jessica was skeptical, but Ronny was forgotten when there was a knock on the door.

The sound ricocheted through her body. She must have ass-leapt three feet off the chair. Thank god she'd set her coffee and phone down beforehand. Jessica set her mug on the table and grabbed both of Ronny's hands.

Projecting her voice toward the front door, she yelled, "Just a minute."

Jessica turned to Ronny with an apologetic look. "Crap, Ron, I'm sorry, I meant to tell you that Clay was coming by, but I needed my coffee first and I thought he wouldn't make it for another fifteen or so. Are you okay, because I can send him packing right now?"

Ronny swallowed repeatedly. It felt like if she didn't, she might be sick or might not be or . . . something. Her palms were sweating, and she was nervous, but it wasn't as bad as yesterday and some of it felt . . . different.

Deep breath in, blow it out. Extracting one hand from her friend's death grip, she patted her right hip. The feel of the metal tucked into a secret pocket in her waistband calmed her ever so slightly.

Not that she planned to whip out her revolver in the kitchen and start firing, it still felt good to touch it. It was an ever-present extension of herself and had been for almost a year.

Interacting with people wasn't her forte in the aftermath, but the week she moved here, she had Jessica take her to pick out a gun. She needed that sense of security so badly, she dealt with people long enough to get trained and get her concealed carry permit. It had felt impossible at the time to be around that many people, but Jess got hers at the same time. Of course, she didn't carry, but she supported Ronny and anything that made her feel safe.

When she went out, she had even more concealed surprises for a would-be attacker. But around the house in baggy sweats and a hoodie, one hidden weapon would do . . . most days.

Returning her hand to the table, she placed it on top of her friend's. "It's okay, Jessica. Let him in and I'll head to my room as soon as he is past."

Ronny borderline laughed at her friend's dumbfounded expression. Jess looked at her as if a second head had sprouted up from her shoulder and started singing showtunes.

"Are you sure, I . . . I don't really need anything fixed *fixed*. I kind of took a screw out of the shelf in my closet and bought a new tub faucet for him to install just so I could take another shot."

Her friend dropped her head onto the table and scolded herself. "I'm an idiot. He doesn't really want me, Ron. Shoot, I don't know if I really want him, I just have this inexplicable need for him to want me. I'm ridiculous."

After bouncing her forehead on the table and calling herself names, another knock interrupted them.

Jessica stood with the bearing of a queen but shouted with the presence of a drill sergeant. "Hold your freaking horses I said." After smoothing down her silk robe, she turned her attention back to Ronny.

"You know what, Ronny, I'm proud of you. You seem so different about having someone in the house and it makes me happy. Since you gave me the go ahead, I'm going to try one more time to get him to notice me. If not, then I'll move on."

Her friend leaned in a dropped a kiss on her forehead. "I love you, Ron. Now," she said and rose back to her full height, which was only around five six, "let's see if he will let me board the Clay Train at least once."

"Ewww. Visual." Jessica rolled her eyes at Ronny's comment and they shared a laugh. She could hear her laughing all the way to the door. It was nice, almost normal.

Ronny considered it a win that her hand didn't immediately drop back to her waist the second the door opened. However, her hold on her mug threatened to send pieces of ceramic into her palms.

Just sip and breathe, sip and breathe. You can do this. A small sliver of the front door was visible from where she sat. She stared intently as Clay entered the house—her house—with a toolbox. Just like . . . *nope, not going there. This isn't like anything. This is this moment and no other.*

The mesmerizing sound of Clay's boots on the hardwood floor stopped, pulling her out of her inner pep talk. She had been staring through him, not really at him.

His attractive blond head leaned into the kitchen opening and his blue-gray eyes were smiling. "Hi, I'm Clay." He threw up that familiar wave, the one from yesterday, but again, she froze . . . except her lips. They turned up in a goofy facsimile of a genuine smile.

Ronny could only imagine how it must have looked. It wasn't like she remembered how to smile.

No way was she ready to engage in conversation but the fact she didn't bolt gave her hope for the future.

Thankfully, Jessica was there to save her from having to respond.

CLAYTON

Holy moly, she was more breathtaking without the sun glinting off a pane of glass.

Even sitting, Clay could tell she was tall, and the fire of her hair was vivid. Half of it anyway—she must dye it because the bottom half was dull. Her lavender eyes captivated him, holding his gaze hostage. Even her forced smile was endearing.

What broke Clay's poetic musing was the glint of uncertainty that bled into those unusual eyes. Not just in her eyes, but her whole bearing.

He'd bet his Ford that if she could have poofed and disappeared like yesterday, she would have. Clay was determined to take her out. He had to, at least once. There was just something about her.

Jessica wrapped both hands around his biceps and tried to tug him down the hall. "Clay, Veronica. Veronica, Clay. Now, come with me please so you can get my closet and tub ship-shape."

If it weren't for the sound of genuine pleading in her voice, he would have sworn Jessica was jealous.

There was urgency to Jess's words that he'd never heard before, so sadly, he heeded them. Allowing himself to be pulled and herded toward her room. "Nice to meet you," he called back over his shoulder to Veronica.

When they were in her designer suite, Clay turned on her a little harsher than he should have. She was not her usual self, sure she was dressed as expected to entice him, but she wasn't flirting. Instead she was pacing and chewing on a blood red nail, muttering about setting her friend back.

"Okay, Jess, I'll get to work, but we're talking about whatever that was and whatever is going on with you when I'm through."

She bobbed her head in agreement. Clay had the fixture on the tub installed in record time. It was a simple enough job and the one Jess chose went well with the tile. Not unexpected considering her interior design degree.

Quickly, he moved to the closet where a shelf hung to one side and most of the clothes had shifted to the lower end. Clapping his hands together around a dozen or so hangered dresses he turned and almost knocked his friend over.

"Here, Jess, take these and lay them on the bed." She turned and did as he bid, freeing his hands to grab another bundle. They continued silently until the rod was empty of clothes and the shelf was void of purses.

Clay examined the support bracket and found just a hint of sawdust and no reason the screw should have come loose. The hole wasn't stripped out and there was no indication the weight was too much for it.

I knew it. Dang it. He thought Jessica had finally got it, but apparently not.

With deep breathing and closed eyes, Clay tried to prepare himself to be mean to the one person he swore he never would be, but nice wasn't cutting it.

Jessica leaned on the closet door frame and saved him the trouble.

"There never will be an us, not even one night, will there?" The relief he felt at the absence of real pain in her voice was tremendous.

Giving her his full attention, he looked into her brown eyes with as much platonic affection and sincerity as he could muster.

"No, Jess, there won't. I adore you, love you like a sister even. And I'm beyond grateful, if not for you, I would have never owned my own business and be where I am today. But no, I don't get a sexual spark with you, and I refuse to use you—in any capacity—the way others have."

Jessica visibly tensed and pulled at her robe trying to cover herself. Clay meant what he said. People used Jess her entire life. People wanted money from her, men wanted sex from her, and some just wanted to be friends with her because of her last name. Not to mention her parents used her to wage war against each other.

Clay vowed never to do that to her. He could have easily led her on and would never have had to pay her back. Even recently he could have slept with her just as an outlet, but he didn't.

It was killing him to know why her family cut her off, but that was a question for another time. Still, it looked like she needed a friend.

A heavy sigh proceeded her words. "Yeah, I've always kind of known it was a lost cause, but you've treated me better than any other man in my life, hands down, and I guess I just wanted that to spill over to other areas."

Clay couldn't resist giving her a hug. There was a hint of something in her voice, but it didn't seem to have much to do with him at all.

"You don't sound too broken up over it. Should I be happy for us or insulted for me?" When she laughed it gave Clay a warm feeling, like she really got it and it wouldn't impact their friendship.

"No insult, I just think I always knew it and maybe I wanted you because of that or maybe . . ." Playful Jess returned so fast it gave him whiplash. "It was thrill of the chase that had me panting after you like the slow gazelle at the watering hole."

Jess turned and went into the bathroom, laughing the whole way.

Clay definitely needed to get her out and about, maybe ply her with beer and get her talking. She had some serious crap happening in her life he could tell. Her upbeat air felt a bit forced, the more he thought about it.

Digging in the toolbox he found his electric screwdriver dead. "Hey, Jess, you got the screwdriver you used to destroy this shelf handy, mine's dead?"

She emerged from the bathroom with clothes on and the screwdriver and screw in question.

"Figure that out all by yourself, Sherlock?"

A raised eyebrow was all she got as an answer.

"Yes, okay, I took the screw out to get you over here. It was my Hail Mary play, and well, it failed. But I forgive you."

"Ha, forgive me? No way, lady, I forgive you. I could be working on my house or Mrs. Wilson's barn, instead I'm here, knee deep in handbags and dresses to fix your shelf."

Jess sat on the floor outside the closet door and watched him. It was obvious she had something to say but he wasn't going to push it.

"I'm glad you're here Clay and I'm sorry I tried to trick you. You're one of my only real friends and I've missed you. When you paid me back and I had no reason to see you, I kind of just stopped trying. I was afraid the only reason you liked me was because of the money."

Clay had figured all that out on his own already.

"I didn't help dispel that myth, did I? I should've kept in touch; that's on me. I didn't even realize you'd moved back here. Last I heard you were working out of Enterprise and were a huge success. I'm sorry I wasn't a better friend."

Shelf back in place, Clay extended his hand and pulled Jess to her feet. Walking her over to the bed they each grabbed a handful of dresses.

Hanging them up together seemed the perfect distraction for Jess. Her hands caressed each dress as she placed it just so.

"Your friendship has never been lacking, Jess." Clay returned for another load of dresses. Handing them one by one to her to hang. "I should've stayed in touch too. I've missed you just as much so let's share the blame for that, okay?"

Her face lit up as she nodded and took another dress. Once the closet was restocked, Clay gathered his tools and turned to Jess.

"Jess?" Clay hated the way her eyes cast downward, presumably at the pity in his voice; even he heard it.

"I heard—" She cut him off with a manicured hand to the air.

"No, just don't. If you want to ask about my family, I'm going to need alcohol, and a lot of it."

With their new boundaries in place, he could do drinks. "Okay, Rusty's at seven. I'll ply you with alcohol . .

. as a friend, and you can tell me all about it." And Veronica, but he left that part unspoken.

"Deal. And I'll be sure to meet the upscale dress code."

The easy laugh they shared to the front door transported him back in time and it was pleasant.

He turned to say his final goodbye and her beautiful roommate stood in the kitchen door. Her height shocked him; she was much taller than he assumed.

"Oh, it was nice meeting you, Veronica. Hey, we're heading to Rusty's for a drink later, you're invited to join us."

Clay tried to dial back the excitement in his voice. When he stepped forward with an outstretched hand, she curled in on herself.

For some reason it hurt him to see that and a bit of protectiveness surged inside him. *I am definitely bringing that up with Jess tonight.*

VERONICA

Having Clay in the house set her on edge, but not as bad as it had been the first time.

She felt like she was finally making progress, or maybe it was just him.

Clay wasn't threatening. Ronny had a hard time even understanding it, but something about him just didn't feel that way. His voice floating through the house from Jess's room didn't set her teeth on edge.

That was the first time in three hundred and thirteen days that a male voice didn't do that.

She'd abandoned her coffee and crept down the hall. Stopping every three steps to take deep breaths to give her time to panic and bail. While her breathing increased and her heart beat a rapid tattoo in her chest, she didn't hit full on panic mode.

After what was likely ten minutes, she made it to her friend's bedroom door and just stood there in close proximity to a man. A man with a tool belt who could easily overpower her if he chose to.

Ronny allowed his voice to flow around her. It didn't terrify her and send her bolting the other direction. It did however cause small flutters of attraction in her stomach.

It's a start. That thought brought a small uptick to the corners of her lips. Ronny wasn't sure it had actually happened until her hand floated to her face and she felt it with her fingertips. The breath whooshed from her lungs and tears sprang to her eyes when she realized she could feel something for a man that wasn't fear.

It was intoxicating. Clay was . . . intriguing. She couldn't put her finger on why, but he was. Listening in on their private conversation didn't flood her with guilt. Jessica would understand when Ronny explained, she would be happy for her, ecstatic.

The heart that had just been trying to escape through her sternum, gave up the effort and stalled in her chest.

"There never will be an us, not even one night will there?"

"No, Jess, there won't. I adore you, love you like a sister even. And I'm beyond grateful, if not for you, I would

46

have never owned my own business and be where I am today. But no, I don't get a sexual spark with you, and I refuse to use you—in any capacity—the way others have."

Clay flat out told Jessica he wasn't interested. Her friend would be devastated. Guilt, a feeling she'd kept at bay for eavesdropping, now hit her like a tidal wave. How could she ask Jessica to be happy for her if she were heartbroken herself?

Ronny wanted this to happen to her, spent months hoping and praying and making deals with any deity who would listen for it to, but not at the expense of her friend. Ronny turned away and rested her back on the wall next to the door.

The full weight of everything all tied together weakened her knees and she slid down. It wasn't all about her and she had no right to make it so. She would suck it up and be there for her friend, it was the least she deserved. But she had to move, had to get away before Jess started pleading.

There was no way she could listen to that or if Jess tried to manipulate him, that would crush her. Most people wouldn't understand that part, but she couldn't deal with it. What if Clay got angry and raised his voice? *No, no, no, no,* she had to move.

Willing her limp legs to support her, Ronny slowly stood and balanced herself with a hand to the wall.

"Yeah, I've always kind of known it was a lost cause, but you've treated me better than any other man in my life,

hands down, and I guess I just wanted that to spill over to other areas."

"You don't sound too broken up over it. Should I be happy for us or insulted for me?"

"No insult, I just think I always knew it and maybe I wanted you because of that or maybe it was thrill of the chase that had me panting after you like the slow gazelle at the watering hole."

The rest of the conversation floated through the open door before she moved away. Ronny couldn't believe her ears; Jess was okay with Clay's rejection. She wasn't hurt, at least she didn't sound it, and Clay wasn't angry. It was a normal conversation between a powerful man and a vulnerable woman and nothing bad was happening.

That did things to her no one else could possibly understand. It was . . . freeing. She hadn't missed the tidbit about Jess sabotaging things to get him over and that didn't sit well with Ronny. But, this kind of therapeutic healing trumped that easily.

When their voices got closer and talk of drinks registered, she forced her legs into action.

She made it as far as the kitchen archway before their laughter was too close to bolt. Instead she did an about face and tried to casually lean against the frame.

Watching them approach the front door she slowed her sawing breath. Clay turned and his eyes rammed into hers. Much like the other day but without the glass barrier. Instead of terror, a tiny zing shot down her spine. The fear was still there, she could feel it clawing at the back of her mind, but she focused on the zap instead.

Moment! First time I've been able to position the fear where I wanted it.

"Oh, it was nice meeting you, Veronica. Hey, we're heading to Rusty's for a drink later, you're invited to join us."

A part of her wanted to scream *yes*, but she knew there wasn't a snowball's chance in hell of that happening.

"Um." Her voice was no more than a squeak. Clearing her throat, she tried again. "Thank you, but, um, I . . ." What was she supposed to say? *I don't go out because I fear crowds, men, loud noises, toolbelts, freaking butterflies.* She was a mess and didn't want to voice it to the first man who didn't send her into a full-blown panic attack.

Pulling her eyes from Clay's was nearly impossible, but when she met Jess's it was downright comical. They were wide and shocked, practically bugging out of her head.

She sent a quick, *please help me look*, to Jess with her eyes or at least she'd hoped she had. Thank god, Jess recovered and answered where her voice failed.

"Oh, Ronny told me she has an . . . obligation later, so she probably can't join us. Right, Ron?"

A bob of her head was all she managed before Jess ushered Clay from her house and she sunk down to the tile.

49

Distantly she heard the soft thunk of the door closing followed by the snick of the screen door a second later, signaling that Clay had indeed left the building.

Her friend skidded on her knees next to her and almost bowled her down.

"Oh my god, Ron. That was huge. You spoke to him. And made eye contact. Holy macaroni. Can I, can I hug you?"

Instead of answering, Ronny threw herself in someone else's arms for the first time in over three hundred days.

The tears flowed without consent from her, but they were tears of release not fear. Tears of a simulation of joy not despair.

She wasn't unfixable. Sure, she was still broken but she could be repaired. Her therapists and her friend all told her that, but this was the first time she actually believed it.

"Crap on a cracker, Ron . . . I can't even tell you how amazing you are." Jess ended the embrace and brought Ronny's face into focus. Through her tears she could see the genuine happiness in her friend's eyes.

"You proved me right. You are not beyond anything. And you know how much I love to be right." Jessica laughed. She was a good person, but serious emotions didn't come easy for her either, so everything ended in a joke. Ronny got it.

"You say that now, but when you realize I stood outside your door and eavesdropped you might think otherwise."

"Shut the front door." Jess pulled them both to their feet and gave her another quick hug.

"You approached a room with a man inside and you didn't panic?"

Her head shook side to side, and she worried her lip. "No, but I violated your privacy and for that I am deeply sorry, I just—"

"No. You don't apologize. That is a huge victory for you, I will not let you taint it or discount it."

Silence reigned for a time.

"So, Clay doesn't scare you? I mean, like other men do."

"No. I can't explain it. The fear is always there, I'm not sure it will ever leave me, but something about his presence doesn't trigger it to take over. His voice is almost . . . soothing isn't the right word, but neutral maybe. It's even attractive, he's attractive."

Jess's jaw dropped.

"Sadly, I don't get all tingly the way I once did over a man I was attracted to, but it's something, right?"

Her friend did a hilarious happy dance. "You bet your sweet ass that's something, something huge."

CLAYTON

Hanging with Jess in Rusty's was like old times, before the games and the loan. It was fun. Jess wasn't exactly the old Jess though in both good and bad ways.

Good because she didn't seem weighed down by the burden of keeping up appearances.

Bad was the snippet she shared about her family. Around the fourth beer she let it slip her family hadn't spoken to her in almost three years.

Something else was weighing heavy on her too, but Clay didn't have a clue. He wanted to help her, let her unburden herself, and selfishly, he wanted to know more about her roommate.

"So, how many more beers do I have to ply you with before you tell me why your family cut you off?" He said it as casual as possible and took a sip from his own drink.

Casual was the last thing he was feeling about the whole situation. There wasn't any reason on the planet to disown a child. Especially one as loyal as Jess. Her parents said jump and she asked how high. The only thing she ever went against them on was Clay.

He wasn't good enough to hang out with, especially not loan money to. *What if . . .*

"Jess, does it have anything to do with me?" He had to believe the answer was no considering it would have been a delayed reaction since the loan was old news.

Jess waved his words off and finished her beer, then signaled for another. "Please, they already handled that when they took away the Mercedes. Two months of begging and convincing them I *learned my lesson.*" She adopted a drunken approximation of her father's voice for the last three words. "They caved and bought me the BMW a couple months later."

With half of her next beer down, she took a deep breath and words started flying out.

"Nope, those assholes cut me off because of something I *wouldn't* do because someone else did *someone he* shouldn't do."

It took Clay a minute to grasp what she said with her drunken grammar. Even though he got the words, he didn't really get their meaning. Apparently, someone slept with someone they weren't supposed to.

"Care to elaborate for me, because I am pretty sure I'm not understanding at all."

Jess raised her beer and talked with her hands, so beer foam splashed everywhere. "My parents decided I should marry the perfect son from the perfect family. I dated Brock and we got along well, and we had chemistry. I think I was even starting to love him, if you can believe that. Me, love someone."

Even though there was clearly more to the story, Clay couldn't picture it. Jess always said she was addicted to the single life, practically allergic to love. She wanted to live life on her terms, but she bowed to her family. She was not the type who fell in love, so it was sad that obviously her story didn't have a happily ever after.

She returned her beer to the bar top after a few sips and folded her arms on the rail. Her eyes met his and he could see the pain they held.

"I thought he loved me too. Anyway, he knocked up the daughter of his mother's maid. My family decided that it was no big deal, they would squirrel us all away in our country chalet—the one my parents were giving us as a wedding gift—until the baby came."

Jess turned away from him and dropped her head to her arms. The burger he'd eaten sat like a lead weight in his stomach hearing Jess speak.

"They expected me to marry Brock, claim I birthed his child, and she would stay on as our maid. Live with the woman my husband slept with and claim their kid as my own in public. It was a perfect plan for everyone. Both families could save face, and I wouldn't have to" —she raised her arms enough to air quote— "face the public humiliation of my husband's mishap."

Clay was at a loss for words. What kind of life would that have been for Jess? How her parents could want their daughter to live that way was beyond him.

Her head shot up and she polished off her beer. "Can you believe that? They care more about public humiliation than me living my entire life being humiliated in my own home. Even worse, Brock said he loved me, and it was a drunken one-time thing and he would never touch her or look at her again. Like that would make having her in my home better."

Clay opened his arms and Jess turned on her barstool and fell into them.

"My parents said do it or you get nothing. So, I took my nothing and left. Well, not really nothing, the car was in my name and I stashed some allowance over the years in a secret account, so I had something. But, honestly, it felt freeing when it was all said and done."

"I bet, sweetheart. I'm sorry you had to deal with that, and I wish I could have been there for you."

"Yeah, me too, but I had Ronny and she helped me through it until . . . anyway, she's basically supporting me now. My money is about dried up and I need to face the world." Clay heard her whisper as she pulled away, "But I don't want to abandon her."

He felt like she had said so much and yet nothing about her mysterious and attractive friend.

Gone were the tears for her parents and her past life. "But that's water under the bridge. I rarely ever cry about it anymore, except when I'm drinking. Anyway, that's why they cut me off. Like I said, I'm kind of over it all now, but with the looming zero in my bank account and the birthday of my kid-not-my-kid coming up, I gave it some mental and emotional space, it's had its due." She brushed her hands and breathed out. "Now it's done."

Jess shrugged it all off and asked the million-dollar question, "What else do you want to talk about?"

VERONICA

Sleep evaded her once again, but not because of rampant nightmares, well, not until the last time she woke up tangled in the covers.

The first part of the night passed with fitful tossing on her nest because she couldn't believe she almost said yes to going to a bar with her friend and a man.

The dreams that interrupted her at first were because she was imagining herself as she was before the attack.

In her dream, she'd danced and laughed with someone on the dance floor like she didn't have a worry in the world. Obviously, being in the house with Clay and not panicking had given her that short reprieve from the nightmares.

Memories assaulted her, but not bad ones. Normal, that was the best description, she was normal for the first time in her dreams since the old her had been viciously murdered.

Having thoughts of a man that didn't revolve around violence was downright euphoric. The last time she'd drifted off to sleep, she saw herself like before, dancing and laughing, but it was with Clay.

He'd gently grabbed her wrist and leaned into her ear to be heard above the pounding music and said something funny. She threw her head back and laughed.

I recognize this night.

Even with the dream like haze, it was memorable; it was her last night as the real Ronny. Her mind simply replaced the guy in the club with Clay, but everything else was the same.

Ronny felt his gentle touch and the kiss of his scotch-laced breath against her cheek as he spoke. His voice was husky and masculine.

After they shared a laugh, he extended his arm like a gentleman asking her to embrace him for the song that had changed from thumping to slow and sensual.

Without hesitation, she stepped forward. Enjoying the feel of their bodies aligned with each other.

Their dance ended, she was out of breath and flushed but felt alive. Her dance partner seemed sweet. He begged her for another dance, and she capitulated. Another dance and another drink and she'd call it a night. She had to work in the morning and had promised herself, and Jess, she'd be home by eleven.

It had been after one when she'd pulled herself away from Colin, that was his name, Colin. She was giddy, he'd asked to see her again and put his number in her phone before she left the club.

The Uber ride to her apartment had been a blur, her mind drifting back to Colin. He was so gentlemanly, even asked before kissing her goodnight. She'd wondered if he could be the one.

When they pulled up to the front of her apartment, she fired off a text to her best friend.

> RONNY: Hey, hooker, made it home safe and sound. Met a great guy, we can dish tomorrow.

> JESSICA: <<< doing a happy dance for you. I'll take my first caffeine run @10. Be there n ready to spill all the juicy deets. U forgetting something, hooker? Proof of life???

Ronny didn't need to ask any questions; she knew exactly where Jess meant. The best coffee in the city had a stand right in front of Ronny's office. It was their go-to since she was the one with a more restrictive schedule.

Proof of life was always required whenever either went out alone. A selfie, at home, at the end of the night.

Ronny's life was almost perfect. A great job, an even better friend, and after the club, maybe a decent guy to share it with.

After she let herself into her third-floor walkup, she took a selfie with her tongue out and a peace sign. It reflected her mood well.

RONNY: There, trollop. I'm tired. C U Next Tuesday. LOL

JESSICA: Forgot Ur Cozy Koala U. LOL

RONNY: Ehhhh, try again, that sucked. Nighty, night, straight wife.

JESSICA: I think it was a solid effort. Nighty, night, PITA.

With a sigh of relief, she kicked off her spike heels, and padded to the kitchen to guzzle sweet tea right from the jug. It tasted weird chasing all that alcohol, but she was ridiculously thirsty after dancing the night away. The tea only made her thirstier though.

Jug in hand, she grabbed her laptop and checked her social media quickly before scanning emails. "Crap." An email from the landlord. He decided tomorrow morning, later that morning actually, would be the best time to fix the stove which had been broken over a month.

Ugh, now I have to get up even earlier. That thought made her groan. She contemplated telling Creepy Carl to shove it and come later, but she really needed it fixed. Plus, he gave her the heebie jeebies so having him there while she was on her way out would be ideal.

Her exhaustion hit her hard and she barely made it to her bed before she was well on her way to dreamland.

Sleeping in a leather skirt, cami top, and full make-up wasn't ideal, but she couldn't muster the strength to stand. Something wasn't right, she shouldn't feel this way after just a handful of drinks spaced out over the course of the whole evening.

A warm and floaty feeling took over her. She found it odd how she felt she could hear things but was asleep, like a waking dream. Her last thought was something is definitely not right.

The sound of the doorbell was a distant, underwater one. "Veronica, you home? I'm here for repairs. I'll let myself inside in sixty seconds unless you respond."

No, she didn't want that creepo in her apartment while she was lying in bed, but she couldn't move. She had zero control over her body.

Panic crushed her when she couldn't get up. She shouted, "No, do not come in, Carl." But it came out slurred and not at all a shout. Turning her head to the side, her phone lit up on the dock, it was just after two a.m. Her mind was moving slow, but when she heard the door close, reality smacked her hard.

Creepy Carl wasn't here to fix the stove at that hour. When he appeared in her doorway, she wanted to wretch. She struggled against invisible bonds to move to no avail.

Thoughts were cycling through her brain, but she could only seem to process every other one.

His announcement at the door was for the benefit of any neighbor who might have seen him, not for her. Why was her brain moving so slow and why couldn't she move?

No, no, no, no, no she chanted in her head as he approached. It was the only word she could grasp as her thoughts trudged through peanut butter.

Able to assert a little control over her muscles, she turned her head his way and flung her arm across her body. "Hmm, you drank more than I'd hoped this time. I wanted you a little more aware, but oh well." He stopped shaking the tea jug and sat on the bed.

As hard as she tried to scoot away, she couldn't make much progress. He lazily stroked up her thigh, touching her in a way he had no right to.

Shaking her head back and forth as much as she could didn't deter him, neither did her slurred no's. He snatched her underwear off angrily from under her short skirt and bound her hands together with them.

As he stood, he placed his phone on her bedside table. While he removed his clothes music floated up from it and her tears flowed.

When he began monologuing while undressing, his words broke her. He recounted how many nights he had violated her privacy. He congratulated himself for his restraint in not consummating their love all the nights she'd been drugged.

She wept as hard as she could, it was the most control she had over her own body. There was nothing she could do to take back the past nor stop what was about to happen.

If only I . . .

Ronny woke with a jolt in the present. It was the final time that night.

The memory was so vivid. It had been a while since she'd had that particular nightmare. For months she had avoided it, somehow steered her dreams, but last night she couldn't.

The only blessing was waking up before . . . She wasn't sure if she could survive reliving that part of the night again. Not now, not when some normalcy was seeping into her life.

Something about Clay felt safe, but she was still powerless. If she couldn't find a way to take that power back, then she was done. Her life was meaningless and not worth drawing breath.

I need to find that power. It felt as if it was so close. With the progress she'd made, and with Clay's presence in her house, repairing it, not terrifying her when he could have, she'd felt hope.

"How can I get it back?" she asked her coffee, but it didn't have any answers.

In the wee hours of the morning, answers didn't come, but she sat there racking her brain all the same.

Hours later, Jess entered the kitchen, the time had passed without answers. She poured herself a cup of coffee. "You're a peach, Ronny, a real peach. Heart of gold still firmly in place . . . check."

Jess joined her and she knew what was coming next.

"On a scale from teenager on Elm Street to Rip Van Winkle, how did you sleep?"

For the first time in a while she had an answer she thought she was done with.

"Teenager on Elm Street."

No sooner had the words left her mouth than Jess asked, *may I,* with her eyes. Ronny nodded and they embraced.

"At first the dreams were pleasant, and embarrassingly involved Clay, but then they changed and . . ." She couldn't finish.

"How far?"

Ronny didn't want to answer, didn't want to validate it, but she had no choice, she had to work through this somehow. "He was undressing."

"Oh, honey." Ronny's body didn't instantly reject her soothing touch rubbing up and down her back. She focused on the feel of her friend's touch, needing to focus on anything but the dream. "That's—"

They both jumped when a knock on the door sounded. As Jess walked toward the front door, Ronny followed, determined to face her fears or die trying.

CLAYTON

Showing up unannounced at his friend's house was stupid. Showing up at said friend's house who was breaking stuff to try to lure him into bed—madness. But he was confident they were past that. They were back on the right path, their friendship renewed, and her attempts to sleep with him finished.

His own home required his attention. He needed to start choosing design elements and a metric butt ton of other things.

Procrastination was the name of the game, he knew it. It was a task he'd always thought he'd do with his wife, but there wasn't a Mrs. Briggs yet. Considering he wasn't even dating anyone, there wasn't one in the foreseeable future either.

Face it, man, you need to suck it up and pick the stuff yourself. Either your future wife will love it, or she could redo it.

So, why was he at Jessica's holding a toolbox and parts for a screen door instead of working on his own home?

Because I want to know more about Veronica.

Their conversation last night had turned to the beautiful broken woman she lived with. Respecting her friend's privacy, Jessica didn't say much, but Clay got enough to know Veronica had been deeply hurt, but Jessica thought he might be the one to break through.

Granted, she didn't come out and say it and she repeated more than once that her secrets were her own to tell but Jess had said he felt different or that Vernonia felt different. It was hard to tell toward the end of the night. Jess had talked in riddles and metaphors.

The haunted look in Jess's eyes when they talked about Veronica spoke volumes. Clay had a pretty good idea how she was hurt—she had the same look his mom once did—he just didn't know how deeply the pain still ran.

In her drunken state, Jess mentioned it had been almost a year and she saw the first glimpse of her old friend after he'd visited.

That was enough to motivate him to first, talk to his mom, and second, head to the building supply store in the early morning hours and pick up parts to fix the catchy screen door.

He didn't know what he could do to help but he was compelled to try. His mom had been attacked at work when he was fourteen.

According to his eavesdropping as a kid, she had fought off her attacker before he was able to "complete" the job as his dad put it, but she suffered a lot of trauma from what he had been able to accomplish.

Clay should have recognized the look, but he was too stunned by her beauty and gut punched by her pain to see deeper. His mom had felt powerless, broken, and found a path back to her strength through rebuilding and repairing, and repurposing appliances of all things.

She'd said, *"There's such a sense of satisfaction from taking something broken and making it work again. As it was intended or as it was destined, either way, it has purpose, and purpose is life . . . it's beauty."*

It wasn't until adulthood that he'd realized that was what helped her cope and live a content life. If he were honest it was also where his love of working with his hands started. She was right, there was power in transformation. Now he wanted to share that with Veronica.

But as he waited for the door to open, he doubted himself. What if she didn't want his help. Jess had mentioned trying for almost a year to help her.

Shaking off his doubts, he set down his tools and started to work. Remembering how things needed to be his mom's idea.

Either way the screen door needed to be fixed and he would do it for them. If the girls wanted to learn, then he would teach them. Together so Veronica could maintain her dignity and her secrets, plus not feel singled out or threatened. Besides, everyone needed basic home repair skills in their repertoire.

Jess opened the front door and jumped back at the sight of him. "Crap." Her hand flew to her chest. "You scared me . . . what are you doing?"

Halting his work, he peered around Jess to see Veronica lingering behind her toward the kitchen, then made eye contact with Jess. On impulse he reached forward, squeezed Jess's hand in greeting, dropped it, and then placed his own in his front pockets so as not to wave like an idiot. "Hi, Veronica."

She dropped her head shyly to her coffee mug but muttered a soft hello to him. He'd take it.

"Sorry I didn't call, but I noticed the screen door needed a little TLC, so I thought I'd not just fix it, but teach you lovely ladies how to do it so you don't have to call someone all the time for minor things. Save you some money." *And maybe remove a touch of that fear from Veronica's captivating eyes.*

He didn't miss the slight shake of Veronica's head or the enthusiastic clapping by Jess. But he didn't react to either, just proceeded to explain as he went. That way they could both hear and learn no matter what.

Surprisingly, Jess not only paid attention but asked questions. She even worked the electric screwdriver, poorly, but it was a start.

Perhaps more surprisingly, Veronica took a few steps closer into the living room and watched intently, studying every move he made. She didn't ask any questions or get too close, but it was something.

"That should do it. We just need to put the stop chain on it and give it a whirl." Jess gave the door a few test runs.

"Nice, and it doesn't make that off-key violin noise anymore. Thanks, Clay." She leaned up and gave him a friendly peck on the cheek then whispered, "Thank you even more for that."

When she pulled away, she cast a quick glance behind her letting him know exactly what she meant. Veronica was just an arm's length behind Jess. She seemed happy with the result, but she couldn't possibly know that was part of his plan, could she?

A soft and lyrical, "Yes, thank you," floated toward him and it punched him in the chest. She was looking right at him for a moment but dropped her gaze and repeated her thanks.

"You're very welcome, both of you." He removed his toolbelt and placed it on top of his toolbox.

"Do you mind if I use the bathroom?"

"No, of course not." Jess sidestepped to let him in. "You want a cup of coffee?"

"Thanks, that would be great," he answered as he stepped into the house. Veronica took a step back, then another, so he stood in place.

Clay used his eyes to hopefully communicate his path. Veronica glanced at him then down the hall, which she was currently blocking. He sure as shooting wasn't going to advance on her, not with that look in her eyes.

The concerned lavender orbs grew large and panicked. Her eyes snapped from him, to the hall, to the kitchen, and landed on Jess begging assistance.

Clay stepped to the right, deeper in the living room but giving her a wide birth to retreat to the kitchen and the rooms beyond. A slight flourish of his hand and her eyes grew even bigger but with a touch less "trapped animal" feel than before.

She gifted him a shy smile, dropped her chin and shuffled down the area he cleared for her to pass. Once she was out of sight, he headed to the john.

After washing his hands, on impulse, he took the tank cover off and unhooked the chain. He replaced the tank cover and almost exited the bathroom before he realized what he'd just done was creepy level expert.

Clay was compelled to help her though. That small smile and her barely audible thanks was like a treasure she'd given him.

Before he could second-guess himself, he turned the knob. Even if he wasn't attracted to her and she never wanted to date him, he still wanted to help her heal.

VERONICA

She hadn't made it past the kitchen when she was attacked from behind. A moment of panic gripped her but then Jess's smell enveloped her and she relaxed into the show of affection.

"Oh my god, I am so proud of you. You had a moment, Ronny, a pretty big one too."

Did I? The realization hadn't fully hit her because of the panic, but she had, and Jess was right, it *was* huge.

Sure, she had to interact with strangers on the few occasions when she left the house, but to interact with a man—with tools even—in her home was monumental.

Placing her coffee cup on the counter, Ronny turned in Jess's arms and returned the embrace, fiercely.

"Oh my god, oh my god, oh my god. Jess, I did. I really did. I can't believe it."

"I can. I told you, you were getting better. Do you believe me now?"

Ronny didn't trust her voice, so she nodded and let her happy tears flow. This was the longest she'd been held since the attack and she didn't have that claustrophobic sensation creep in like usual. Which had her squeezing her friend a little tighter.

A throat cleared in the direction of the living room and they ended their embrace, but Ronny didn't shrink back or make a poor attempt to hide behind her much shorter friend.

After she dashed her fists under her eyes to clear the tears, she raised her gaze to Clay. But that is not what stunned her. It was how she held his gaze for a few breaths.

"Thanks again," she squeaked out before retrieving her cup and using it as a shield.

"You're quite welcome. I'm going to head out. I've got some work to do on my house and an entire afternoon to myself, so I plan to make the most of it."

Jess approached and ushered him to the front door. Ronny found herself following at a distance. Closer than she'd been to Clay before and when he turned to say his final goodbye, she got caught up in studying him.

His eyes weren't as blue as she'd initially thought, up close they were more grey than blue. They almost glowed against his tan skin and sharp jaw.

She appreciated the way the sun reflected off the reddish tint in his strawberry blond hair. It was shaved close on the sides and long on the top reminding her a little of a Viking. Clean shaven had always been her type but the scruff he sported was masculine and didn't overpower his jawline.

Ronny absentmindedly took a sip of cold coffee and recoiled. Not just at the ick factor of the drink, but the realization that she was appreciating him as a man. She waited for the panic that didn't come and she smiled.

Clay's head pitched to the side and met her intense gaze. With a little wave, he said, "It was nice officially meeting you, Veronica." And then he smiled that smile. The one she saw across the yard in the waning sun. She lost all control over her facial muscles and returned it.

Jess had turned around and the stunned look on her face gave away what had happened before her brain had even processed it. Her hands flew to her lips before she could even blink. Sure enough, that was a smile.

Shock overtook her and her eyes shot back to Clay's as he dipped his head shyly, squeezed a stunned Jess's arm, and turned to go.

The sound of the door closing sounded like it came from under water, so did her friend's singing voice. "You really liiiiiike him. You think he's cuuuute." She was dancing around, if what she was doing could be called dancing. Ronny laughed at her friend's silliness and the fact that she wasn't wrong.

Jess stopped singing and did a happy dance all the way to the refrigerator.

"Sit," she ordered. Standing on her tiptoes and reaching over her head to the liquor cabinet above, she asked, "Tequila or spiced rum?"

"Jess, it's not even lunch time."

She turned an indignant gaze her way. "I don't care, you've had a major day already and we're going to celebrate. I can only reach the front bottles without a stepstool, so I ask again, tequila or spiced rum?"

Ronny stood and reached around her friend for the orange vodka, handed it to her, and shooed her out of the way. Opening the fridge, she turned to her best friend with orange juice in hand. "At least we can pretend we aren't drinking hard liquor before lunch."

Normal.

Ronny hadn't felt this normal in so long, as if day drinking was normal.

Well, it's kind of was an occasion and, no, dang it, this is an occasion and I am going to enjoy it.

Turning off her mind, or at least lowering the volume, she sat down with Jessica and drank. A lot of giggling and toasting ensued, but seriousness was never too far away, not for Ronny.

"Do you think you'll be ready to try to live again soon?" And there it was. Had it been anyone else asking,

Ronny would have felt judged at how long it was taking her to regain herself.

But that wasn't why Jess asked. Her friend was genuinely concerned for her. Not in a *hurry up because I want my life back too* way, but more an *I love you and I want you to be happy* way.

For the first time, she had an honest answer that wasn't I don't know. "I think I'm making strides that I haven't made before." Ronny set her glass down and took both of Jess's hands in hers. "I think I want to try, small steps of course, but I genuinely want to attempt things I've been fighting hard against, and you are a huge part of that."

They sat that way for a while, just watching the tears swirling in each other's eyes. "Let me clarify." Releasing her hands, Ronny refilled their glasses and took a healthy swig.

"I've always wanted to, it was just, I wasn't willing to take a risk to make it happen. I just realized that today. I paid lip service to finding my old self, but . . ." Trailing off, Ronny looked for answers in the orange liquid, but none were to be found swimming there in the pulp.

"I mean, I did all the exercises, kept the journal, but when it came to going out" —she waved her hand toward the front of the house— "and doing things that scared me, I refused. Now I see that in order to really start that journey, I must step outside of my comfort zone, literally."

"Ron, I hope you know I'm only asking because I love you and want—"

She cut her best friend off. "I know, and that's why I can see it. If you weren't patient and didn't want it for me when I couldn't, I'd never be ready. Thank you. And having Clay in the house helped. It gave me sweats and shakes, but it is teaching me that it doesn't have to end badly."

Her throat went dry as memories assaulted her.

"Drink up, lady. Drink until we pass out. The doors are locked and we're safe. Drown those demons for now and we can wake up with a horrible headache and cotton mouth to remind us why we don't do this often."

CLAYTON

The rest of the day, Clay walked on air. The almost inaudible thank you and genuine smile Ronny gifted him that morning was like a ray of sunshine that followed him all day. A warm ray just for him.

The days he spent working on his own house were the best. It was down to the details now. The smell of the fresh paint was comforting as he installed the hard wood flooring.

Standing, he wiped the sweat from his brow. His house would be ready to move into in a matter of days. He was looking forward to hauling the old trailer away and getting the front yard landscaped.

His eyes drifted across the open floor plan to the spacious kitchen. He'd chosen basic white cabinets and grey granite counters for the kitchen and baths. Yet, he was going to move in with no cabinet hardware and the most basic of faucets.

Choosing the backsplash, flooring, and paint were a breeze compared to hardware. "Charlie, do you think I'll have hardware before I move in?" His friend stopped his task and stared at the cabinets too.

"Nah, I think Roscoe will win Best in Show before you pick that dang hardware."

At the mention of his name, Roscoe P. Coltrane quirked his head in their direction and lazily opened his eyes. He lost interest in two seconds flat and rolled over. .. then promptly farted and went back to sleep.

Clay chuckled thinking how Roscoe would never win anything but a stinkiest contest. Regardless, he loved that bassett hound like a child. A smelly furry child. He'd always planned to be married before he finished his first home. Design would have been his wife's area.

Clay, you need to get a grip on life, it's just cabinet and drawer pulls, it's not defusing a bomb. Jess had studied interior design in school, he could ask her. Thinking of his friend turned into thoughts of Veronica. The idea of asking her opinion brought a smile to his face.

That smile fell as memories of what he'd done assailed him. Borderline stalking behavior. That was not who he was, and he didn't want that dishonesty looming, marring anything and everything moving forward. He wanted, no that's not right, he was compelled to help Veronica, but not like that.

After wiping his hands, he pulled his phone from his pocket. Charlie was already back at work installing flooring at a pretty good clip, so he stepped out to make a phone call he really didn't want to do but needed to.

Jess answered before the first ring ended. "Hey, Clay, I was literally just dialing your number, our hall toilet isn't flushing. I was hoping you could give us a—"

"I know." Those two words had an edge that cut his tongue, but it was nothing compared to the shredding his confession would do. He'd do less damage if he'd chewed on razor blades.

"I-I disconnected the chain earlier. I just wanted . . . I can't explain it, I wanted you to call me. I feel like Veronica . . ."

His words trailed off, how could he explain his need to help a virtual stranger, to see her thrive and to just see her without sounding like a class A creeper. All he needed was a white van and a lost puppy or physical impairment.

"Hold on," Jess whispered into the phone and then everything went silent. Clay checked the phone display to see if she'd hung up, but the call was still active, so Jess must have muted him. "Okay, spill," his friend demanded.

She sounded muffled and odd. "Where are you?"

"I'm in my closet because I don't want Ronny to hear, she was in the bathroom with me when you called and sound echoes in there. Now, stop stalling and spill, why break our commode and what do you feel about Ronny?"

She didn't sound angry, she sounded almost hopeful. Clay took a deep breath and went for the kill with total honesty.

"The other night when you were drunk, you spilled some truth about her, no details, so you didn't betray her trust, but enough that I know something really bad happened to her and you feel helpless and can't stand watching her just exist in this world."

A soft sobbing reached his ear and tore at his heart. "I love her, Clay," she sniffed, "I love her like my own blood, and I shouldn't have said anything, that's her story to tell. But I'm relieved a little too, but what does that have to do with the toilet? And be honest, I think I know, but I'm a bit of an emotional mess today, not all bad."

Jess really was a good soul. "Because when my mom was attacked, learning a trade, fixing things, helped her find herself again and I thought, maybe . . ."

He didn't need to finish; it was obvious what he'd done and Jess's sobbing increased but had a different tone to it.

"Clay, you . . . you are just, well, you know I adore you and, to be honest, I was happy when I found it broken."

What?

"How are you so happy about me destroying your stuff in order to spend time with a chick I barely know and who's not for me?" The last four words came out barely a whisper. Not because he had great love for Ronny. Sure, he found her attractive, but she didn't fit his life plan. He'd always dreamed of a strong life partner to stand tall beside him and take on the world.

He didn't mind vulnerability. He'd hoped his girl would possess enough to come to him and draw strength from him. But Ronny was different, Clay didn't get the sense she was ready to be that person for herself, let alone anyone else.

That didn't stop him from wanting to help her get there. It was a downright compulsion to do so, but he'd no romantic illusions of anything ever developing between them. It would be welcomed, but he was a realist.

Clay was patient with most things, but his ten-year plan was already behind schedule. He was so deep in his head he forgot he'd asked a question until Jess answered.

"Because, you may not have noticed because you don't know Ronny like I do, but she was a different person while you walked us through fixing the door." A heavy sigh sounded through the phone. One laced with sadness and hope. "I glimpsed the old her, just a small peek but it was beautiful."

He didn't know how to respond. "You did that, Clay. She's been a shell of her former self and for a few moments, she felt whole standing next to me. After you left, I had my best friend back for a wisp of time. Different, but still her."

"Wow, I don't know what to say." Clay saw it work with his mom but to be a part of it was something else. "I'll be right over, but I won't deceive her or you again. It's wrong for me to break things. She has to come around on her own."

"Agreed, *you* can't break things, that's no way to start a relationship. I'll see you in a few. Love ya."

"There is no . . ." he'd started to say but Jess had already ended the call.

VERONICA

Shockingly, she found herself anticipating Clay's arrival. She wasn't hiding down the hall or even curled around herself on the fringes of the room.

Greeting him at the door was probably not going to happen, but baby steps. Anticipating a man in her house without a boatload of anxiety was a step in the right direction.

What she'd felt yesterday was nice, but she wanted more. Observing him fixing the door and teaching her made her want to grab a wrench and tighten something or loosen it. Just change its state.

As silly as it might sound to normal people, which she didn't consider herself to be anymore, there was something powerful about having the ability to change something so much.

The screen sagged and squeaked, now it didn't. Clay had done that. Changed it, fixed it. *Controlled* it.

Yeah, I don't sound crazy at all.

Still, she decided she would step into the closed space of the bathroom with Clay and learn how to *control* a toilet.

The low rumble of his truck sounded in the distance. It was a somewhat familiar to her already. Well, most things were, even if she only heard them once. Side effect of what had happened to her.

Most days she was hyperaware of her surroundings to the point of paranoia. It had gotten better over the last few months, but it would always be a part of her.

However, for the first time, she took a result from a horrible, unspeakable act and embraced it. Being hyperaware wasn't an altogether bad thing.

Like now, as she padded to the window, peeked through the frilly curtains, and watched as he pulled up in front. Clay shut off his truck and stepped out onto the lawn, then reached back into the driver's side and lifted something.

She squealed before she could stifle the sound as a bassett hound appeared in his arms. Clay gently set the lazy dog on his feet and she could tell he was still technically a puppy. His floppy ears had her oohing and ahhing. Clay turned and retrieved his toolbox and closed the truck door.

He clicked his tongue and the puppy happily trotted along beside him. Ronny dropped the curtain and forced her legs not to give out. She wanted to rush to the door and snuggle that cute little face. That terrified her. Not that Clay felt threatening but that her safety wasn't in the forefront of her mind.

It was that disregard that could get her hurt again. Jess had opened the door and the dog greeted her with a low mournful woof.

"Oh my god, that must be Roscoe. He's adorable." Jess sounded as enamored by the puppy as she was.

"Yep, Jess, meet Roscoe P. Coltrane. Roscoe, meet Jess. He can hang on the porch if that's okay. He's too lazy to run off, aren't ya, boy."

Ronny rounded the corner in time to see him bend down and ruffle the dog's fur. She hadn't planned on speaking, but dogs were magical.

"Roscoe P. Coltrane, like The Dukes of Hazzard cop who had a bassett hound named Flash?" She was laughing, actually, laughing. Stunned by the fact that she. Was. Laughing.

Apparently, she wasn't alone, Jess's jaw was practically on the floor and Clay's eyes were the size of half dollars.

Without preplanning or over analyzing, she dropped to her knees and Roscoe trotted to her immediately. He dropped to his haunches, tilted sideways, then his head was in her lap and belly exposed.

Clay stepped in and the screen door shut with a small clack behind him. She didn't panic as he entered. His voice brought her attention away from the belly rubs she was doling out.

"Uh, yeah. Kind of a huge Dukes fan. I've seen every episode at least five times." He'd dipped his head shyly and rubbed the back of his neck. It was an endearing look and she felt a tiny piece of her protective coating chip away and trickle down to the metaphorical ground.

"By the way, sorry for springing him on you. I didn't plan on him invading your house."

Jess answered for them, but she agreed. "No worries, Roscoe is welcome anytime." Ronny had returned her attention back to Roscoe, but she saw Jess squeeze Clay's arm and tell him, "As are you."

What struck her most was the way Jess touched and interacted with him. It was so different than before. She didn't seem to be interested in Clay any longer, not in a sexual way anyway. It was a relief because Ronny hated any kind of manipulation and when Jess wanted something, she wasn't above taking any means necessary.

That quality made her a fierce and loyal friend, but sometimes she went overboard. It did her heart good to see that she wasn't doing that with Clay anymore.

"Well, let me see about that toilet. You ladies want to join me to learn how ridiculously easy toilet repair is?"

Ronny nodded but was tied up in bonding with her new best friend.

"You both can pay me back for the lesson with an opinion, if you don't mind. I'm having trouble picking hardware for my cabinets. Torn between classic country and industrial chic."

They trailed him into the small space. Her breathing became shallow, but she bent down and buried her hand in Roscoe's fur to help calm her irrational fears.

Dogs were amazing creatures, Roscoe seemed to sense what she needed and took a protective stance at her feet. He sat regally right on her toes, looking at Clay as if daring him to make her flinch.

A giggle escaped her at the ludicrous thought of his own dog turning her protector in a matter of minutes. But the idea helped her breathing even out and that's what mattered.

"Ronny would be the best to ask about design, I worked *for* a design firm, she worked *with* one. Big difference, I was nothing more than a glorified secretary. She was all the rage back in Enterprise."

That snapped her attention up from the multi-color fur that held her gaze. "Please, I was barely employed and far from being a rage of any kind."

Her hand flew to her mouth before she could tell it not to. She'd voluntarily spoken to Clay, or Jess but with Clay right there. Either way, he hadn't rushed her or made an aggressive gesture. Even his handsome features were somewhat relaxed but slightly stunned.

Was he as shocked as she was? If so, he recovered much quicker. The smile that split his face was downright blinding and gave her butterflies, but not the dread kind.

"Perfect. I have a few samples, a catalog, and pictures of my kitchen with me. I'd love your input after I finish up here."

The hopeful expression on both their faces had her nodding in agreement. She wanted to rush to Jess and give her a big thank you hug because she would be there every step of the way as she'd been all along. Not to mention she brought this man into their lives.

The scrape of the porcelain as he removed the tank lid set her teeth on edge, causing a shudder down to her toes. Roscoe whimpered and looked up at her.

No longer able to resist, she bent down and retrieved the healthy pup. He was an armful, but worth it. She buried her face in his neck and took a step closer. Although he didn't fit the mold of a guard dog since he was practically already snoring, she felt safer with him in her arms. Clay explained how a chain connected the lever to a flapper valve. The chain was lying on the bottom instead.

Jess leaned in and asked, "So, it just looks like the chain came loose, so no need for new parts, right? Just a quick reconnect and we are master plumbers. Woohoo."

Everyone laughed at that. "True, but since we already have the lid off and it's probably been a while, we can go ahead and replace the flap if you want. I brought one with me."

"Then we'll be master plumbers?" Jess wasn't letting go of the joke. "I can buy loose jeans and walk around with my butt crack showing?"

"Not exactly, and whatever floats your boat. I can print you a certificate of achievement if you want but you're on your own with the wardrobe upgrade."

CLAYTON

Distracted by Ronny, it took him too many attempts to connect the chain. Her laugh was addictive. One taste and he would give almost anything to hear it again.

Roscoe was cradled in her arms like a baby and it felt . . . right to see him there. A twinge of jealousy tried to steal his joy as they exited the bathroom, but he fought it. Roscoe never allowed Clay to hold him like that, not for long anyway.

He loved to lounge in his lap, and belly rubs, but he always got stiff and uncomfortable if Clay tried to carry him too much. The hound was anything but uncomfortable in Ronny's arms. His head swayed back and forth with every gentle step she took, tongue lolling to the left. Roscoe was out like a light, not a care in the world.

Clay increased his pace reaching from behind to give him an ear scratch. Before he was within a foot, his soulful eyes popped open and stared straight into Clay's. Almost daring him to touch him. *Hmm, not as out as he appeared to be.*

I'll be, Roscoe was protecting Ronny. He sensed her distraction and didn't want her startled. It was the only explanation since he didn't have a mean bone in his body, and he loved ear scratches.

Ronny turned and headed for the couch. Sitting slowly, she lowered Roscoe to her lap. Completely lost in his dog, everyone else ceased to exist.

The constant fear etched on her face was dulled. The tightness around her eyes, the set of her jaw, and her ever-tense muscles bunched and ready to bolt. All those things changed, all the tension subsided.

It was the first time he'd seen her like that, and she was stunning. He'd thought he had no designs on her other than being helpful, because she didn't fit his plan. He'd always dreamed of having a partner with a take no prisoners attitude. A woman who devoured life like he did.

When he first saw her there was a physical attraction but that was all he allowed. She needed to find herself, be just Veronica before she could be someone's girlfriend or wife. The clock was ticking on his well-ordered life plan, though.

There wasn't time for him to wait for someone to rebuild her own life so they could start one together. But, right there, in that moment, he decided he could put that plan on hold for a woman like her.

If she was the one for him, the wait would be a small price to pay. Only one way to find out if that's the case, and that's to help her find her strength, her power, her sense of self.

She was worth the delay, even if it didn't work out for them as a couple.

The only part that stuck in his craw was Jess would be right. She'd never let him live it down. She must have seen the change in Ronny or maybe it was the change in him, because she applied a quick death grip on his wrist before letting go and dashing her cheeks.

"Clay, why don't you put your tools away and grab the hardware sample and whatnot? I'll grab us some snacks and lemonade."

"Uh, yeah, sure." He turned his attention back to Ronny. "Do you mind holding onto Roscoe for a bit longer while I grab some things from the truck?"

"Sure, I'd love to, right, boy." She was rubbing his head and talking to the dog but answering Clay's question. That was good enough for him.

Snatching what he needed from the truck, he turned back toward the house when his phone vibrated.

Crap, he muttered to himself. It was Rebecca, his date for Saturday.

Clay was so focused on his timeline that he finally asked her out. She worked at the home store and they'd flirted for months. She was attractive and witty with a touch of snark, totally his type. Yet for some reason, he never pulled the trigger on a date.

She'd recently finished up classes and was promoted to manager. Again, totally his type. Go getter and she was ready to settle down. Rebecca's hints had gotten less subtle but that wasn't exactly a turn off for him.

Strength was his weakness. He loved a woman who knew what she wanted and went for it, as a rule, the opposite of Veronica.

Suddenly it hit him, he only asked Rebecca out after he'd met Veronica. It all started making sense; he was attracted to her from the moment he glimpsed her in that window. But when she didn't tick off his check boxes, he'd practically ran to the home store to ask Rebecca out. Like he was trying to prove something to himself.

Jesus, I am pathetic. His attraction to someone different than his preconceived notions caused him to panic. Was he so devoted to his timeline that he could hurt people in the process? When the answer was obviously yes, he hated himself a little.

He didn't have the courage to take the call yet, so he let it go to voice mail. He'd cancel on her in person, it was the right thing to do. Clay wanted to see if his attraction to Ronny was because of his need to help her or because he was genuinely into her.

It's the second. He already knew the answer. Heading inside with a rock sitting in his stomach, he accepted that no matter what happened, his timeline was busted.

When Clay re-entered the living room, Jess was already sitting on the couch next to Ronny and a plate of grilled cheese sandwiches, a yellow bag of chips, a jar of pickle slices, and a pitcher of lemonade sat on the coffee table. How long was he outside and lost in thought?

Taking the chair across from the ladies, he laid his burden on the table next to the bag of chips.

Jess slipped forward and started doling out food and drinks. Ronny seemed more interested in Roscoe than food. The dog had other ideas. He slinked from Ronny's lap and curled up at her hip.

Everyone seemed focused on their food until a semi-disgusted, "Seriously," broke the silence. All eyes turned to Jess, and she gestured between the two of them with her bitten triangle of sandwich. "I can't believe there are two of you. Gross."

His eyes clashed with Veronica's violet ones before dropping to her plate, then back to her heart-shaped face. Her jaw mirrored his in a fly catching position.

Each had the top layer of bread peeled back from their grilled cheese and had loaded them with potato chips and pickles.

All he could do was stare and laugh. He'd never met anyone who ate like he did. Ronny asked him in a shocked voice while making eye contact, "Do you eat your hamburgers with only ketchup and french fries too?"

Clay was rocked back in the chair, it was the first time she'd spoken directly to him, or so it felt. He nodded. That was exactly how he ate them. No mustard, no cheese, just ketchup and a crisscross pattern of fries.

"Wow. How is it that I know two weirdos like y'all?"

"Just lucky, I guess," Clay answered and dove into his perfect grilled cheese.

When they were through eating, Jess cleared the coffee table of food and drink, and Clay spread out his stuff.

"His kitchen is lovely," Ronny said to Jess and handed her the pictures of it. She was back to speaking through someone else, but it didn't bother him. He got it, really, he did. She'd spoken to him earlier and they connected. He would hold on to that and hope it would happen more often.

"Perfect layout for function and fashion. You did good with the colors; they mesh well and give off both masculine and feminine vibes." Her attention was absorbed in the pictures and she looked strong and confident as she studied them.

"I agree," Jess chimed in. "That's a very hard balance to achieve. Kudos to you." She set the pictures down on the table and scooped up the catalog. Thumbing through it, she continued, "I always knew you were in touch with your feminine side, and it shows. I bet the rest of your place is just as amazing."

Ronny slapped her hand on the catalog as Jess flipped the pages lazily. "These." She took the booklet from Jess and extended it toward Clay but laid it on the table as he reached for it. It seemed it might be too much of a connection for her.

"The brushed steel will flow with the appliances. The soft edges are feminine and the small diamond cuts add a touch of masculinity," she told her lap.

VERONICA

Ronny shuffled into the kitchen in her fuzzy unicorn slippers. Jess was at the coffee maker pouring two steaming cups of the heavenly smelling brown liquid.

There was a zing of excitement—one she'd long forgotten the feel of—anticipating Jess's routine question.

She wouldn't say the peach line as Jess had woken up before her and made the coffee today.

"So, on a scale from Rip Van Winkle to teenager on Elm Street how did you sleep last night?" Jess didn't turn, just continued doctoring their cups of coffee.

Ronny suspected she wasn't expecting the answer she was about to get. If she were, she would have been Irishing up those coffees.

"Well, I didn't exactly grow a grey beard, but the only thing that woke me up was the call of my bladder." The tinkling of the stirring spoon halted abruptly. The only difference between her friend and a mannequin at Macy's was her choppy breathing.

The urge to hug her friend from behind was overwhelming. She embraced Jess like they used to do to each other whenever one needed some girl chat time.

The second her arms landed around Jess's stomach, she crossed her own over Ronny's and gripped them with the strength of Arnold Schwarzenegger.

They stayed there and silently enjoyed the moment as their coffees cooled. Jess finally released her death grip, so Ronny grabbed both cups and turned toward the microwave.

While they waited for the beep, they didn't speak, just stared at each other. The joy was evident in Jess's beautiful brown eyes.

They sat together and sipped their coffee while making small talk. No mention of Clay or home repairs, just the normal chatter of two old friends.

It felt liberating. Somehow more so than if they'd made a big deal of things. They'd made a huge deal of it actually by treating it like it was—*there's that word again*—normal. The fact that it happened was big enough and Jess was saying so much by saying nothing.

No longer able to contain herself, Ronny blurted out, "I miss design."

"Of course, you do." Jess gave her a look that said, well, duh. As much as she knew about the inner working of Ronny's mind there were still plenty of secrets.

Lies.

Fine, she argued with herself, *lies*. Little tiny ones that were for Ronny's sake and Jess's.

Lies that made others feel better so they'd stop asking how she was doing and when she was going to get back to life, etc.

Taking a deep breath, she decided to fix one right now. "No, I mean I really do miss it. I know I've always said I would go back and whatnot, but in all honesty, that was nowhere near the truth. I never had the slightest urge to do that."

A sip of caffeine was needed to push on. "Design was, is . . . pure poetry through flow and function. Beauty in a raw form to me. That was something I knew I couldn't embrace. Beauty had no place in my life anymore. Not to mention that was part of the old me. The me I never wanted back, no matter what I told you or the therapists or anyone."

Jess surprised her by grabbing their cups and shuffling to the coffee maker for refills. No judgement, no visible disappointment, just Jess listening.

The shuffle of her slippers on the tile was a comforting sound. After she sat with one leg tucked under her backside and the other knee propped up, she asked, "What's so wrong with the old you?"

Leave it to Jess to dissect her words and get to the meat of it all. "The old me was great, but I've blamed her for so long, I don't know if I can ever love her again." Jess's lips formed a protest, one Ronny silenced immediately.

"I said blamed, past tense. In the last year, I've learned to not take the blame for what happened. Yes, I was dressed a certain way and still drunk from the night before, but it wasn't my fault, I get that. But I can't forget the way I'd felt every day about her. So, while I don't blame her—me—now, I can't seem to forget that I did and all the real, raw emotions I felt. Wrong and otherwise."

A sad smile passed her friend's lips but it quickly turned into a genuine one. "Well, I think that's great."

"The design part?" Somehow even though she'd been the one to confess, she felt she was missing something.

"Yes, of course that, but even better is you called the past you *her*. If you can't feel complete and utter love toward *her*, I'm glad you have separated the two in your mind. To me, that means you are kind of grooving the new you. One that has been . . . is being slowly born over the course of the last . . ."

Jess's words trailed off and her eyes widened. Her hand flew from her cup to her mouth just as a squeal erupted, startling Ronny.

"Oh my god, you haven't counted. The last few days, you haven't counted."

"Counted?" Ronny whispered in a confused voice.

Jess popped up like a jack-in-the-box and grabbed her from her seat and hopped around in a circle holding her hands in hers.

Infectious was the only word to describe Jess's elementary school celebrations. She was still unsure what they were celebrating but enjoyed it all the same.

"Yeah, counted." Her voiced wobbled with her motion. "You said a year, that's an estimate. You said attack, a direct reference, but no three hundred and however many days. No stopwatch, no timer counting to reference. It's lost some power because you didn't BC and AD it like you've done. That deserves a happy dance."

The spring left her on the next gravity assisted motion. No bouncing back up, a boing without "ing." Just the "bo."

Jess didn't know how accurate she was. She *had* lost count, even in her head. Sure, she could pull it up quickly, but the information wasn't right there waiting for her to think of and reference. Happy dance indeed.

That's a moment.

She reached for Jess's phone in her robe pocket and Jess lost her "ing" too.

"What?" She didn't want to really tell her friend that the only playlist she had was to distract her when needed. There was no music just for fun on her phone, there hadn't been since she'd lost her love of music that night too.

A shudder racked her body as a memory assaulted her when her eyes landed on one of the titles. A song he played from his phone on the bedside table while he'd attacked her.

"Hey, where'd you go?" There was concern in Jess's voice as she shook her gently.

With a deep breath, she scrolled past the offensive song in search of something with a little beat. After hitting play, she toggled the volume up and dropped the phone in the decorative bowl in the center of the table to project the sound a little.

As the music started, they danced around like they used to. They'd spent many a night at each other's place doing just this. Dancing around. Usually with wine and pizza while sporting some hideous facial mask to shrink their pores, because they were classy like that.

After they'd exhausted themselves with impromptu dancercise, they heading to the laundry room to catch up on the weekly chore. Ronny usually completed the task during her bouts of insomnia. But that was one of the drawbacks of sleeping better, the laundry piled up.

Grabbing her pile of folded clothes, Ronny surprised herself yet again and kissed her friend on her cheek. "Thank you."

Two words which were barely audible but held so much. That was it as she headed for her room. But not to hole up for the day, as would be her usual, but to shower and live.

Maybe she would go out and tend her grandmother's roses. Or fire up the old lawnmower and give the yard a much-needed trim. She could even see herself in the garden readying it for some vegetables. The sun blinding her as it set, sweat dripping from her brow. Dressed in some sweats and a loose tee, she headed to the shed and a fresh start. Along the way she noticed Jess was still in the laundry room and she gave a small smirk as she passed.

"Where ya headed?"

"I think I'll do some yard work today."

She left Jess slack-jawed and bounced outside.

CLAYTON

"**P**retty darn good, and yourself?" Clay answered Mrs. Wilson's inquiry as she kept pace with him heading to the goat barn. For a little old lady, she sure was spry.

"I can't complain much, although I'm sure I still will." She chuckled under her breath and Clay couldn't help but join her. Other than being set in her ways, she wasn't a mean person, just full of fire. As his dad would say, she got up and drank piss and vinegar for breakfast.

"So, Mrs. Wilson, what can I do for your goats today?" He bent down to pat one of the black goats on the head. He really liked them and thought one day it might be fun to have a few.

Mrs. Wilson stopped when a brown and white goat trotted right up to her and head butted her thigh. Clay thrust his arm behind her before she lost her balance and ended up on the ground.

"Oh, Thomas, you cranky old cuss," Mrs. Wilson scolded, but there was nothing but love in her voice. She turned her attention to Clay. "I need you to run a fence there along the yard up to the barn, and all the way through."

"So, you want me to divide the yard and the barn in to two separate areas?"

"Yes, that's exactly what I meant. I need to have Thomas and his main lady, Agnes, separated from the rest for a while."

When she bent to scratch the white goat that had loped up, she explained further. "You see, I want Thomas and Agnes here to have babies this season so I'm going to breed them."

Curiosity got the best of him. "I don't know much about goats; do they have to be isolated? Is that bad for the breeding pair?"

"No, it's just that I want to make sure that little Thomases and Agneses are the only possibilities when she comes into her cycle. Since I can't be out here watching them all the time, if I separate them, they'll do what comes naturally. Then, in about five months I'll have beautiful baby goats."

All righty then, that was more than he wanted to know about goat breeding but hey, a paying job was a paying job. "Well, lucky for us, this looks like a pretty straightforward job, Mrs. Wilson. Since you already have two separate barn doors with a divider, I'll run the fence right up between the two. Then I'll do a separate divider for inside. It shouldn't take me more than a week, or if you let me bring in Charlie, we can have it done in two or three days tops. What do you think?"

Clay saw the look of disapproval creep into her rheumy old eyes. "Mrs. Wilson, before you answer, Charlie works way cheaper than I do and if you let me work with him, then I'll charge you his rate for both of us instead of mine. Plus, we'll be done in half the time. It's a win-win. Less than half the money and time. What do you say?"

It was obvious the minute she was ready to capitulate. She lived on a fixed income and since her husband passed, she didn't have a lot of help. Charity wasn't something she'd accept, but she would bargain. Most jobs he did for her, he only charged his expense for parts and supplies. Plus, anytime anyone hired his company it was the same hourly rate no matter if it was Charlie or Clay who showed up. She didn't know about any of that or she'd skin him alive.

Besides, Charlie needed to build a rapport with the people of this town so they would start letting him do some of the repairs. If Mrs. Wilson trusted him, others would follow suit. Maybe one day Charlie could branch out on his own. There was enough work for both to be successful.

"Well, Clayton, you got yourself a deal. You and Charlie can start whenever. I want it done as quick as possible so Thomas here can start to court Agnes properly."

"Okay, Mrs. Wilson, I'm going to take measurements now and see what materials I need. If I can get them all at the home store, we can start tomorrow. If not and I have to order them, it could take a few days."

Mrs. Wilson gave one last nod and turned back toward the house. As Clay started taking measurements, he halted her retreat with a question. "What do you plan to do with all the baby goats?"

"Well, I was thinking of selling them as pets. You know, make a little bit of money and make some people happy. Let's face it, goats make people happy."

Clay chuckled; he was in total agreement. There was something special about goats. "How much will the baby goats go for, if you don't mind me asking?"

"Depends on who's asking," she answered with a twinkle in her eye.

"I'm asking. Roscoe needs a friend and he could do way worse than a goat."

"For you, Clayton, I'll give you first pick and it won't cost you a dime. You've always been good to me. I know you think I'm too old to see what you do but I'm not so old I don't recognize good deeds. You don't charge me near as much as you charge everybody else in this town. I know that for a fact, and I know why, because I'm stubborn about those things. But you've allowed me to keep my dignity and my goats and you've never once told me no."

Clay was getting a little choked up.

"It'll be my pleasure to give you first pick and see you love your goat the way you do that silly old dog of yours."

She turned and made it to the house with surprising speed before he could even protest. A little piece of him wanted the goat for Veronica. The way she'd embraced his dog and opened up around him made him think a goat could help her too.

Of course, you didn't go getting people gifts that they had to feed. He'd always wanted a goat, plus he had forty-five acres and a love for animals. A goat wouldn't be the only one in his future.

Clay finished up his measurements and headed back to the shop. He saw Charlie's car at Rusty's, so he popped in there instead.

"Hey, boss man," Charlie greeted as he walked in. "I just ordered lunch, you hungry?"

"I could eat."

"Hey, Rusty, can you add another burger basket?" Charlie called to the back.

"Of course, I can." Rusty looked through the cutout to the kitchen. "The usual?" Clay nodded. Rusty knew how he ate his hamburgers and always humored him. What would he think if he knew there were two of them?

"So, what did Mrs. Wilson want?"

"She's going to breed goats, so we've got to divide up part of their yard and barn. Shouldn't take more than a couple days if we work together."

"Yeah, well, she doesn't want me near her house, so I guess it'll take you a little longer than a couple of days, but I'll handle the other jobs so you don't have to worry."

"Actually, she wants us both there." The shocked looked on Charlie's face made his day.

"Really? She specifically invited me to do a job at her house? Around her goats, and she's not gonna sit out there with a shotgun giving me the grumpy face all day?" Clay and Rusty busted out laughing.

"Wow, it's like you've lived here your whole life. You know her well. Let's just say I made her an offer she couldn't refuse. I stopped by and the store has everything we need, should be ready for pick up soon. We can start in the morning."

"Cool. I finished up the flooring in your house, so you're ready to move in. Have you given any more thought to hardware?"

Before he could answer, Rusty delivered their burgers. Charlie shook his head as he took a bite of his cheeseburger loaded down with everything from tomatoes to the freaking kitchen sink and pointed at Clay's food with his.

"How can you eat that, man? You know it's weird right?"

"You call me weird, but you have like twelve condiments on a cheeseburger. To me, that's weird.

"Well, to each his own," Charlie said as he took another bite.

"As far as your hardware question goes, yes, I've decided. I'm going to order it when I go pick up Mrs. Wilson's fencing." The bite of burger Charlie had been chewing almost fell from his mouth when his jaw slacked.

"Seriously?"

"Yup."

"After months of indecisiveness, that's all I get—a yep?

"Yep."

"God, I hate you sometimes."

He was still swallowing the last bite of his burger with ketchup and french fries when his phone rang.

Pulling it from his packet, he didn't even bother checking the display.

"Hello?"

"Hi Clay, what do you know about dryers and lint flying around the laundry room like a swarm of bats?"

A laugh bubbled up from his chest because he could practically hear Jess flapping her arms at lint bats through the phone.

"First, turn the dryer off. Second, look behind it and tell me if the fat silver tube is split or detached from the wall or the dryer?"

He waited while she complied.

"Yes."

"Yes to which part?"

"All of it. Please help?"

"Okay, easy enough fix. I can grab parts, is tomorrow afternoon soon enough? I have a job to get started in the morning."

"Works for me. Another lesson deserves pay in the form of dinner. Thanks, Clay."

Suspicion crept up his spine. "One more question, Jess. Was the dryer fine this morning?"

"Yes." And she hung up before he could even react. She'd said it would be deceptive if he broke stuff, but not her.

"You sneaky devil," he whispered as he ended the call on his end.

VERONICA

Ronny woke when with her bladder about to burst. After going through her typical morning routine, she actually looked at herself in the mirror.

Like really looked.

The dye in her hair had faded more than she'd previously allowed, and her natural red was blazing through almost to the tips. She had no desire to re-dye it right now. She was starting to love her natural color again.

Instead of hiding it under a hoodie she combed it to a perfect shine. Catching it up in a high ponytail, it felt foreign, grooming for appeal rather than function. It had been so long.

Even more out of character, she changed out of her pjs before heading to the kitchen for coffee.

Jess wasn't standing at the coffee maker waiting to ask her how she slept. It happened that way some mornings, but today felt different. Panic rose and started to choke her, she turned to run down the hall to check on her friend and came to a dead stop when she saw her curled in the chair reading a Sam JD Hunt book.

Taken by Two. That used to be one of my favorites, but my love of reading was collateral damage. Seeing Jess enjoying it sparked a hint of jealousy. *I want to curl up and read like that again.*

"Well, hello Rip," Jess spoke with humor lacing her words as she bookmarked her page and closed the well-worn copy.

Jess raised the book toward her before placing it on the coffee table. "I hope you don't mind, but I borrowed this when I went to check on you. You were out like a light and it was just sitting in the top of the box calling my name."

Check on me? Why would she check on me? And, why was the sun so bright this early, and . . . before she could pose another mental question, she whipped her head to the old grandfather clock. It was after ten.

"I . . . I slept in?" Confusion and disbelief, and a million other emotions assaulted her. She never slept in, never.

"Yes, ma'am, you sure did. So, can I assume Rip Van Winkle is definitely the answer today?"

"Yeah, I guess it is." Her voice shook. "But regardless, I still need coffee." She turned on her heel and went straight for caffeine.

The urge to toss out the exact number of days it had been since she'd slept in wasn't a compulsion as it would have been just last week.

There was a mental reset when she'd quit counting the days. Speaking and thinking about it in a more general time frame stole back some of that power.

It wasn't just that. Or rather, that didn't stand alone. Clay had something to do with her progress, something big. It felt nice to know she could duct tape something back together or what not. Power and strength.

That was the one of the strange things coursing through her body while she waited for the dripping to stop. The other was attraction. She was seriously attracted to Clay.

Jess followed her into the kitchen and leaned against the door frame. Her stance was almost smug and she crossed her arms across her chest. "So, you slept well, you flat ironed your hair, and"—she sniffed the air—"is that perfume?"

Busted. Turning from the counter with steaming cup in hand, she blew once and took a sip and answered, "Yes, yes, and yes. I wanted to feel a little normal today and so . . ." She gestured to herself and plopped into the chair Jess usually sat in.

It was exhilarating being unscheduled and unrestrained. Just living. She wanted that feeling every day from now on.

"Do you plan on going anywhere?" Jess quizzed her as she sat down next to her.

"Well, I am working up the courage to head to the home store, if you'd come with me, of course. I want to pick a new color for my room. I can't say I'm ready to paint it just yet, but I am ready to entertain the possibility with samples."

"Wow, I was not expecting that answer, but heck yeah, I'm in." Jess knew the significance of the paint samples but was sweet enough not to point it out. It was on the list. The list one of her therapists had her make of signs she felt were markers on her road to recovery.

It was a silly practice, or so she'd thought, but she'd made the list and her therapist advised her to share it with someone she trusted. Sleeping through the night and painting her room were some of the signs she never thought she'd see.

Even though she wasn't sold on the importance of it all, she was sold on giving it all a try. In the beginning, she'd complied so *when* it failed, it wouldn't be on her because she gave it a try. It had been horrid reasoning but the important thing was, she'd maintained and updated the list as time marched on.

Her eyes shifted to the drawer it was tucked away in. A place Jess could read it at her leisure without them having to discuss it.

The latest update was before bed last night, so she doubted her friend had seen it.

"Oh, I forgot, Clay is coming over to fix the dryer hose. Would you be okay with him alone? I have an appointment, but I can totally cancel if that isn't something you can't do yet. We can still go to the home store afterwards, regardless."

Before she realized what was happening, her breathing had increased, and her stomach got fluttery. It was confusing because only a miniscule part of it was panic, the other part was the thought of seeing Clayton.

Ronny didn't fear him in the same way she feared other men. Clay had been nothing but non-threatening. He even moved from blocking the hallway when she felt uncomfortable. She liked to think that was because he understood her somehow. Like they had a connection.

I'm ready to take a leap. I'll either crash to the ground in a broken heap or I won't. Either way I'm moving forward today!

"What time do you have to leave? I think I can handle it if you're here to let him in when he arrives. I'm okay with being here with him but I don't know if I'm ready to open the door and invite him in, if that makes sense?"

Jess leapt up and pulled her into an embrace. "It makes perfect sense. I'll be here as you need me, you know that. Can I just say I'm happy for you? You're stronger and braver than you even realize."

Thank god she'd taken a few extra minutes when she got up and wasn't standing here in fuzzy slippers and ratty pjs, because the rumble of a truck announced Clay's arrival moments later.

Jess released her and made her way to the front door. Ronny rinsed her coffee mug and smoothed down her clothes. A smile split her face when she heard the soulful howl of a bassett hound.

Before she could turn and walk to the archway, Roscoe was trotting up behind her like he owned the place.

"Well, hello handsome." She greeted her furry friend and stooped to give him scratches behind the ear.

A pair of work boots were right behind him. "Well, thank you. I'm not used to being greeted so nicely by my customers, although I did get an impromptu marriage proposal once after I located the smell that had been plaguing her AC unit for months. You do *not* want to know what was causing it."

Clay's eyes were down right sparkling with humor when she raised her attention from Roscoe to clarify who she'd been talking to. No need, it was obvious he was joking, and she'd almost missed the social cues.

Standing, Ronny clasped her hands together, mainly because she really had no idea what to do with them other than pet the dog.

126

"You're right, we really don't want to know," Jess said before Ronny could even open her mouth.

For once, she'd wanted to be witty and clever. Engage in the banter normal people engaged in.

"Well, I have an appointment, are we all good here without me? As much as I need to learn how to fix a dryer, I really do need to run." She made her way around Clay and grabbed her purse from the counter. A gentle grasp to her biceps had Ronny looking down into the brown eyes of her friend. She whispered, "You good? I can stay."

Ronny didn't trust her voice yet, so she laid her hand atop her friend's and gave it a squeeze as she nodded once.

Jess turned to head out and said, "Why don't you record it for me, Ronny? You can give me a play by play and it will be like I'm here." And she was gone.

Emotions swirled inside her like feathers in a twister. The full range of the human experience was attacking her. Every extreme one could think of was warring inside, but above it all, Jess's words rang out over and over.

I love you to pieces, Jess, you're too clever by a mile. She'd given her a measure of security. By telling her to record it, she was telling Clay to behave himself, not that he needed it, but she knew that reassurance would give Ronny some peace. Not only that, she was giving her something to focus on if she needed a distraction. An important task, a diversion from panic.

Meeting Clay's gaze was tougher than she'd expected, but she did it anyway. There was no judgement there, even though they'd stood in awkward silence for god knew how long while she quieted her demons.

It was almost understanding that swirled in those grey-blue depths. If she didn't know better, she'd think Clay knew her history. She staggered back, *that wouldn't be the worst thing in the world.* She kind of wanted him to know.

"Would . . . would you like a cup of coffee?" The squeak in her voice didn't thrill her, but she focused on the warm furry body literally sitting on her feet instead.

Roscoe was a perfect distraction from her racing heart and disjointed thoughts. *My own personal therapy dog.* The thought warmed her heart.

"That would be nice, if it's no trouble." Clay made a forward step motion and she held her breath. He paused and she let it out. "Is it okay if I set my stuff on the table?"

"Sorry, it must be heavy, yes."

CLAYTON

It was obvious there was a war raging inside her. Clay recognized the signs easily. *God, how many times have I seen that look on Mom's face?* On rare occasions it still crossed her face.

Waiting until he had permission to step forward, he relieved himself of his toolbox. Placing it gently without marring the finish on the café style table.

"May I sit?" He didn't really need to sit, but it would put her in a position of power. Give her warning if he moved. The sound of the chair would give him away. She had to turn her back to make coffee, yet she stood staring at him.

It was late for coffee, but he could use the extra energy.

Once he sat, she slowly turned and gave him her back. There was a slight tremble in her hands. Clearing his throat before he spoke, so as not to spook her. "So, you've known Jess since middle school, right?"

"Yes." Okay, so she was not volunteering any extra information. He knew the story already of how they met when Jess switched schools and then how they reconnected later, but he wanted to hear it from her.

Veronica turned and set the cup on the table and then slid it toward him before stepping back to her original position leaning against the counter. Roscoe stepped back into his station as guardian.

He drank his coffee in awkward silence. *So, small talk is out.* She was clearly uncomfortable with this one-on-one interaction, so he gulped down the rest of his coffee so they could get to work.

"Well, I guess we should get to it. Are you ready to fix a dryer?"

"Yes."

"Okay, point me the right direction and let's see what we're working with."

When she pointed rather than stepped forward, Clay rose and took the lead. It made sense in his head that she wouldn't want a man following her down the hall. A wave of anger washed over him. Someone purposely did that to her. The anger he felt wasn't just for her, it was for his mother and for every person in the world who'd suffered such a thing.

People shouldn't feel that way in their own home. Home means safety and security. The place you can be yourself without worrying about the outside world, but that wasn't the case for his mom or Veronica. They would always see home differently than other people. It would never be a hundred-percent haven. Best case scenario was to get that percentage as high as possible.

Even though it had been decades since his mom's attack, she was at a solid ninety-five percent. There were still and would always be things she did differently, but his mother lives a full life and he hoped Veronica would too.

Grabbing his toolbox, he headed down the narrow hallway she'd indicated.

"On the left," she said.

He turned as she instructed and holy moly. The laundry room was massive—bigger than his bedroom in the trailer. There was a long folding table built into the wall with cherry wood cabinets above and below. A large chest freezer, a utility sink, and of course a washer and dryer lined the walls. There was room for two more of every appliance if they wanted to double up.

"Wow, all you need are some wired baskets with hanging rods and this could be a laundromat."

Ronny laughed, like a genuine humorous laugh from behind him. "Ahem."

Clay turned and she pointed to the alcove behind the door and sure enough, there hung a wired basket with hanging rod. Along with a professional clothes press.

"I stand corrected, this is a laundromat." He turned back toward the dryer. "Well, let's see what's going on with the dryer before you lose customers." The laugh he elicited from her was soft, more of a giggle. She dropped her gaze to her feet as her cheeks pinkened.

Reaching to turn off the gas before he jostled the dryer, he saw the problem immediately. *Subtle much, Jess?* The vent hose had been detached from both the dryer and the wall, plus it'd been cut. No way that just happened. Jess was playing matchmaker and he kind of adored her for it.

"My grandma was fiercely independent and refused to use a laundromat, even though she couldn't maneuver through the small area."

Crap. He jumped when her voice sounded right behind him and bumped his head on the wall. Luckily, he kept his curse inside or he might have startled her.

Clay peeked out from behind the dryer. She was sitting cross-legged on the folding table with Roscoe curled up at her side. It was the most she'd spoken to him since they'd met.

"Gram hired a contractor to make this room maneuverable for her. They knocked out the wall and expanded it through the small bedroom that used to be there. She used a walker most of the time, but she planned for the eventuality of ending up in a wheelchair. That's why everything is spaced the way it is. It's accessible to walkers, wheelchairs, and scooters."

There was pride in her voice when she spoke of Mrs. Jackson. He chanced another peek, her posture was relaxed, her face was . . . content. She loved her grandmother, but there was a hint of something else there.

"She was a very smart woman. It's a very efficient layout." He kept his voice soft.

"Did you know her? I mean, you did grow up in the area." His mom knew her well, but he wasn't sure if she wanted to hear details. He liked that she was talking to him and didn't really want to slow that down with a long explanation.

"Yes, I knew her, I think everyone did. She didn't abide strangers. You either already loved her or you would by supper time."

The laughed they shared was more than a giggle, and it held meaning. "She actually said that to people, you know? When she met them. As a way of introduction. If they extended a hand, she'd grab that hand and pull them in for a hug and say, '*I'm Sophia, and don't go getting bent out of shape 'bout the hug, you'll love me so much by supper time, you'll be hugging me.*' People didn't know how to react to her half the time."

"I bet. She weighed a buck ten soaking wet, but I can see her muscling full grown men into hugs." No longer able to resist, he pulled himself from behind the dryer, and sat against the wall. When he looked up, he caught light glinting off one of her cheeks. The glistening of tears.

Her face said happy and the tears said sad. It seemed she felt things strong and in extremes. *Always warring.*

"You really loved your grandma, you miss her a lot. Some days more than others." Clay was speaking from experience.

Ronny raised her lavender eyes to meet his gaze and he was struck yet again by her unique beauty. Was it wrong that he hated her tears but loved the way they added facets to her eyes? What he didn't like was the way she picked at her nails and dropped her gaze to her lap.

"I used to spend so much time with her. She taught me how to cook, crochet, can, garden, you name it. If it was a skill, she had it. But when I got a job in the city, I quit visiting as much."

She shook her head and the red reflected in the fluorescent lighting in the room. How had Clay never met her? It was a small town, and everyone knew everyone else. Maybe because his mom retreated after her attack and he didn't get out much after that. Instead he stayed close by her side as her protector.

A memory of him being at this house when he was small scratched at the back of his mind. He was reaching for it until she spoke.

"And instead of being angry with me, she was understanding every time I had to cancel. Then after she passed and they gave me the note she left with her will, I felt like the worst failure. She wanted nothing more than for me to be happy and if that meant not hounding me for avoiding her, well . . ."

Veronica spoke few words, but when she did, she revealed so much. Her entire body changed as she spoke. At first, it was with confidence and fondness. Then it slowly morphed into regret and self-blame. Even though she'd stopped speaking, she had so much more to say. Clay just sat there silently. Giving her the venue she needed if she wanted to continue.

What came next grabbed his heart and tried to wring every drop of blood from it with a twisting wrenching motion.

"She left me everything, including this house. She wanted me to come home. Her house was always more home than my parents' and she knew it. She wanted the happiness and joy she got from planting her roots here and tending her roses for me. Gram practically begged me to come back, set up a design firm, and be the caretaker of all she had."

Her voice broke and that shattered something in him. Clearing his throat he wanted to speak, but what could he say?

"She always did know best. If I had moved here after she died and left the house to me, I wouldn't have been . . . wouldn't be . . . like this." The last two words were barely audible but were a shotgun blast to the gut. He physically curled in on himself before he could stop.

There it is.

Veronica blamed herself for being attacked. She didn't exactly say it, but he heard it anyway. It took every ounce of control he possessed not to jump up and wrap her in his arms and tell her everything was okay.

The only thing he could think to do to pull her from her downward spiral was distract her. "If you'll grab a wrench from the toolbox and come stand so you can see behind the dryer, I can teach you how to replace this vent hose."

With his back braced against the wall, he pushed the corner of the dryer forward so she could see from farther away. "Oh, and don't forget to record it for Jess." Clay liked how her face changed when he suggested that. It was a safety net for her. What he didn't care for was the haunted look that still clung to the edges of her eyes.

With the wrench extended toward him in one hand, the ding of the recording sounded from the other. "May I?" Tipping his head to indicate the wrench, she nodded. Clay reached for the tool and just barely brushed her fingertips. Not gripping, just touching. Ronny didn't flinch away, just stared at where they were connected.

"You know, I like you the way you are but if you want to change things, I have no doubt you will." He hoped it didn't come out like he liked her scared or that she should change. He just wanted her to know it's okay to be in transition.

Before he could muck it up even worse, he took the wrench and began to explain the simple procedure of replacing the vent hose.

"You should check this" —indicating the hose and the vent hole— "and this regularly. Lint can build up and present a fire hazard."

He worked and explained at the same time. "Tighten the hose clamps to finger tight. You don't want lint flying about, but if you go too tight, you can crush the connection here." He pointed where and was done, but Ronny was still standing close by. Hesitant to simply stand and spook her, he patted the side of the dryer. "Now, I just need to slide this puppy back in place, being careful not to kink the hose, and it's a job complete."

At the sound of the word puppy, Roscoe raised his head and woofed. It was perfect timing. Ronny made her way back to the hound, set her phone down and scooped him up as if he weighed nothing.

VERONICA

Extremes. That was where she was bouncing today. Back and forth, back and forth.

She had the best sleep last night since the attack. It was even late when she'd woken up.

I guess almost a year of non-restful bites of sleep can't be remedied by 6 a.m.

She'd welcomed a man into her house, a man with tools and nothing bad had happened to her.

Unless I count wanting to kiss him stupid, which is ridiculous.

She'd spoken out loud about her Gram and her shortcomings as a granddaughter. But at some point during the day, she'd accepted that Gram didn't blame her. Maybe it was the way Clay spoke fondly of her.

However, the most shocking development of the day was that Clay touched her and she'd allowed him to. *I actually wanted him to.*

She couldn't wait to watch the video on her phone. She'd turned the camera to their hands. Now she wanted to see the proof.

It didn't seem real, yet too real at the same time. Ronny buried her face in Roscoe's fur as she left the laundry room and headed toward the front of the house.

Clay was behind her. She stopped in her tracks when that realization hit her. It wasn't even a thought to let him walk out first like she'd done when they entered. She just snuggled the dog and put one foot in front of the other.

The smile she felt on her face and in her heart was monumental. It wasn't that she'd thought to walk in front, it was that she hadn't thought at all. This man was somehow repairing her while fixing things around her house.

It sounded downright ridiculous, but he was. Or rather he was giving her the means to fix herself. It was like he somehow just understood. She wanted to bare her shame to him, and her soul.

I want him to know he is special. I want to know him, period.

Ronny spun so fast, Roscoe's ears helicoptered out beside him.

"Do you like to eat?"

What?

"Wait, I mean do you eat . . . like, lunch?"

Still not nailing it, Ronny.

"I mean" —she took a calming breath and closed her eyes— "do you want to eat lunch here?"

Ronny opened her eyes and turned to the front door. Changing the subject, she said, "He needs to tinkle, maybe." Roscoe had started to whine so she walked right out the front door and set him on the front lawn.

Pacing and chastising herself, she occupied her mind while Roscoe strolled over and sniffed one of the hydrangea bushes. While Roscoe watered the plants, Ronny caught sight of Clay at his truck.

As he hefted the toolbox over the side of the bed, his muscles pulled taut against his flannel shirt. The man was well-formed, and she'd have to be dead not to notice.

She kind of had been just that, dead-ish. But now it felt like she was awakened from that dead-like state. She started dreaming of a future . . . among other things. Such as turning Gram's house into a design studio like she'd wanted her to.

The way the afternoon sun cast shadows on his face, played up the sharp angles. Clay ran his hand through his strawberry blond hair. The sweat caused it to stick up in messy spikes, highlighting the shaved sides.

Definitely Viking vibes, her thoughts caused her to blush. He tilted his head to the side and down as he approached, stopping out of arm's reach.

Roscoe's business was complete, so he loped over to his owner and Clay rewarded him by stooping down to dole out pets.

"I would love to have lunch here. I smelled it when I first walked in and my mouth was watering the whole time. What's on the menu?"

He stood and seemed to be waiting to be invited back in and that was awkward. "Um, I'm not sure. Jess started the InstaPot before I got up. I guess we should go see together."

Ronny reached down and snatched up Roscoe. For some reason she felt like she could do it with him in her arms. Her own furry shield and confidence booster.

Taking the steps tentatively, she paused for too long on each, but Clay hadn't moved yet. Roscoe licked her face and it spurred her on.

Entering the house, she left the door open but the screen was slowly closing. Once she was in the house, she snagged the crochet throw from the back of the chair. In the kitchen, she placed it along the wall and gently sat Roscoe atop it.

Watching him circle his little crochet nest before lying down reminded her of her own nightly routine.

The soft snick of the screen door alerted her to Clay's entry. "Can I come in?" Since he was in the house, he must have been asking permission to enter the kitchen, her space.

"You're a very perceptive man, you know that?" she confessed but nodded and extended her arm toward the chair.

While Clay sat, she turned her attention back to Roscoe. She smiled as he was already softly snoring, belly in the air and ears flopped out. Roscoe's circling and her own nesting reminded her of a movie she saw with a talking dog. He said he was building a mind fence. Which now made sense.

Clay's stomach chose that moment to rumble. She had a hungry guest, and that gave her something to focus her attention on.

While the pot vented, she grabbed some plates. When she was able to remove the lid and the full facets of the aroma hit her, she smiled. "Well," she said as she traded the plates for bowls. "Looks like I chose poorly and Jess chose perfectly." She smelled the bowl she'd ladled out. "My favorite."

After she filled two bowls full of chicken and dumplings, she set them on the table along with spoons and turned toward the refrigerator. Without asking Clay what he wanted to drink, she poured two glasses of three fourths sweet tea and one fourth lemonade.

When she returned to the table, she set the glasses next to the bowls and took the seat opposite Clay.

His gaze on her was intense, like a physical touch. She wanted to get lost in his eyes and swim in their depths for a while. Weightless and worry free, but it was too intense.

Dropping her line of sight to their lunch sitting equidistant between them, she reached for a glass and bowl. After she'd loudly slid them across the surface, Clay retrieved his, his gaze not faltering until the steam hit his face.

Just because she couldn't hold his gaze, didn't mean she wasn't still studying him beneath her lashes.

A look of joy overtook his features as he took a long inhale of the fragrant soup. The action sent the butterflies in her stomach into a frenzied flight. His half smile showed just a hint of his straight white teeth.

Thank god she wasn't staring directly at him because it was blinding. He expressed happiness with such abandon she was almost jealous.

"This smells like my childhood." He took a healthy bite without blowing on it. Immediately, he was fanning his open mouth and making the ha ha ha sound.

Shooting iced tea from her nostrils was not how she envisioned this going, but that's exactly what happened.

After he'd cooled his mouth, his humor seemed to increase. "So, it's like that, is it? Laughing at my pain already? I'd say as far as lunch dates go, this one isn't exactly stellar, but the company is still flawless." He took another drink and she paid rapt attention to his neck as he swallowed. His Adam's apple bobbing with the motion. "Except that you find joy in my agony."

So lost in him, she almost missed his words.

"I . . . date? I'm sorry . . . I mean. I shouldn't laugh, and—"

"Ronny, relax, I was joking. I found it funny too. But I'd still like to think of it as a date of sorts. Is that okay?"

"Yes." *Oh my god, did I just squeak?*

"Excellent." Clay took a few more bites before wiping his mouth on a paper towel. When he was done, he extended his hand, palm up across the table. It just laid there. Not moving closer, not closing or pulling away, it was just . . . there.

Her eyes refused to look up. With his other hand, he continued to eat his chicken and dumplings. Looking down at his meal, rather than her.

It emboldened her. Casting her eyes directly on him she studied his strong forearm which should have been too close but wasn't.

Tracking her gaze upward, again she noticed his biceps testing the ability of the flannel to hold them. His strength which at first was a point against him now seemed to have swayed in his favor.

Not once had he tried to use his size to intimidate, direct, or control her. He wouldn't even muscle past her in a narrow space.

An involuntary dreamy sound escaped her as her vision traced the line of his neck to rest on his too perfect face. Clay had hit the genetic lottery. Sharp angular face, a masculine face. Well-formed nose, kissable lips, high cheekbones, and eyes with such depth they really were windows to his soul.

What she saw there was rearranging her learned behavior and teaching her that her thinking had been flawed since her attack.

He had to feel her gaze, but he didn't look up. Just continued to eat in silence. Clay really was a very perceptive and decent human being.

That thought had her hand inching slowly toward his. Voluntary but safe contact. When her fingertips brushed his, he stilled and so did she.

Clay recovered quickly. Stunned at the realization she craved a man's touch, *this* man's touch. Something she hadn't discovered until she took a chance.

Focus still on his meal, Clay spoke softly. "I'm a good listener. I don't judge and I won't even comment if you don't want me to."

Whoa. Could she talk to this man? There was doubt assaulting her from all angles except her fingers. Her fingers were grounded because of him.

Maybe she could start small. Share . . . something.

CLAYTON

Clay was swimming in disbelief. He hadn't expected her to take him up on his offer. His line of thinking was offer and offer and offer, and eventually she would come around. Like dealing with a wounded animal. Slowly build up trust and eventually they let you look at their wounds.

Instead, Ronny was touching her fingers to his. Not holding on, but reaching out, connecting. So much more than he'd expected on multiple levels.

Not only had she blown him away with her acceptance of his offer, it was almost sappy and magical. Like something made for Hollywood. That touch was unlike anything he'd experienced, and he wanted more.

"You seem like a fixer, not a listener." Oh, he knew the last thing someone like her wanted was to be *fixed*. But she was spot on, he *was* a fixer, but in her case, being a listener was the way to allow her to fix herself. *So, I can still be a fixer and not lie.*

With his gaze still cast down, he chanced a quick glance at her but she wasn't staring at him. She was staring at where they were connected.

Apparently, she was as shocked as he was.

"I am a fixer, but where is it written a fixer can't be a listener? They aren't mutually exclusive."

Clay leaned back in his chair and pushed his empty bowl forward without breaking their contact.

"Why don't we try this? You ask me a question and if you feel I'm not completely open with you, you don't share anything with me? I'd like to get to know you, Veronica. Not just the beautiful parts, and I hope you'd like to know me."

Watching the understanding settle into her warmed his heart. He suspected no one had said that to her in a longtime.

"Are you real or do you live in book somewhere? Most people avoid the ugly and those who don't, well, they're either paid to listen to it or they see the beautiful differently after. So people tend to make inane conversation because they really don't know what to say."

When she pulled her hand away, he wanted to snatch it back and reconnect to her. As much as it bothered him, she had to share her way. He left his hand there regardless.

"Even Jess. She's my best friend and a person this world is lucky to have. But as much as she tries to see me the same, she doesn't. Not that it's bad, it's just different."

"But life is ever evolving, both good and bad. No one sees anything the same forever, no matter what. Our experiences shape and mold us. Reforming our outlook on life constantly. Tell me, do you see Jess the same way? Or even me for that matter. From that very first day when you saw me through the window to this moment right now, do you see me the same?"

Please say no, please say no.

It was with a shocked voice she answered. "No. I don't. Everything is different. I was so focused on how things changed after I was attacked, that I lost sight of how things *always* change."

Her dainty hands flew to her mouth and her eyes widened to an impossible size as tears clung to her bottom lids.

"I don't know why I said that. That's not what you need to know or I need . . ." Ronny dropped her head to her knees which were visible between her and the table. He hadn't even noticed when she'd put that barrier up and that's precisely what it was.

"Don't ever apologize for feeling or speaking those feelings. Of all the things that can be taken from us, the way we feel can't. We get to control that, no matter who might wish it otherwise."

There was no answer from her mouth, but he knew she accepted his words as truth when her hand slithered across the table in search of his. Clay leaned forward and put his directly in her path.

This time, she curled her index finger around one of his. She wasn't just touching, she was holding.

"How is it you seem to understand me when no one else does? They try, but it never really seems like they get the things I do. Yet you seem to read me right away."

There was still no eye contact, her head was down, staring at an unknown spot below her.

Navigating this was going to be tricky. He needed to be completely honest with her or risk her closing off. But at the same time, he didn't want to out Jess and what little she told him.

"My mother was attacked when I was younger. I don't know the extent of her assault as far as all the details, but I know it was bad."

"Was she . . ." Her voice had gone soft. Timid and horrified but sympathetic at the possible answer. A word she couldn't seem to speak aloud.

"Yes." That one word racked her body with a shuddering sob.

"I'm sorry, so sorry." Her grip on his finger took on a boa-like quality and he returned it without thinking.

"Don't be sorry. She wouldn't want that. It's not how she's wired. Besides, things in the past are set in stone. There's no changing them. The only thing we can change is what we do with it moving forward."

Clay didn't expect speaking about it would be so hard, but it was.

"My mom lost almost two years of her life after that. Nothing brought her joy—not me, not my dad, not anything. Watching her every day almost broke my dad. Nothing or no one could pull her out of the memories of that day."

"What changed?"

"She found a way to pull herself out and as she did, she taught me to fix and build things. Said it gave her power over something. She could see a broken fridge and knew she had the power to make it not broken. Her passion was refurbishing and repurposing. Would you like to hear what she said about it?"

Ronny slowly raised her head and nodded making sporadic eye contact with him.

"She said, *'There's such a sense of satisfaction from taking something broken and making it work again. As it was intended or as it was destined, either way, it has purpose, and purpose is life . . . it's beauty.'* I think she was speaking more about herself but either way that stuck with me."

It was adorable how Ronny's jaw dropped. She got it and for a split second, he understood something else his mom said. *"There's a positive to be found in everything, you just have to know where to look and be brave enough to see it."*

There was a *positive* in Ronny telling him those things, he stared into the lavender proof at that moment.

And as much as he refused to credit it all the way back, there was something to what his mom said.

"You asked how I *got* you, well, I saw the same something in you that stole my mother from me for two years. And I have to tell you, since I promised openness, Jess did indicate something had happened involving you when I asked, but she didn't tell me details. I could tell it bothered her. Deductive reasoning, I guess."

Clay hated the anticipation. Waiting to see if she would release his hand. If she would be upset with Jess. *Note to self, give Jess a heads-up just in case.*

"I'm sorry." He eased his grip on her finger and her head snapped up, pinning him with her unique gaze.

"I'm not. Are you sorry bec—"

"I'm sorry because I feel like I invaded your privacy somehow." He didn't like the defeated edge to his voice. It sounded as if he'd already given up.

"Your complete honesty is refreshing. I know people walk on eggshells around me. People who notice something is off about me anyway. No one is ever mad at me or mean to me. It's like they think I can't handle it. Jess is the only one who tells me like it is . . . for the most part."

The sigh of relief went bone deep. She was so much stronger than even he'd realized. She was exactly the type of woman he needed. He'd almost missed it because he'd written her off. Ronny was strong, she'd just forgotten it herself.

His mom's lessons applied to other areas too. He was looking at Ronny, and he was *seeing* because he was brave enough to.

They talked for hours. Two fingers hooked together and leaned over a table. She didn't mention the attack again, and that was okay with him. He liked getting to know her on a level that had nothing to do with any significant life events just random stuff.

His obsession with *The Dukes of Hazzard*, her obsession with naughty romance books. His love of action movies, hers with B movies. Both their appreciation for design with clean lines and elements.

It was their shared reverence for the truth and disgust for lies that turned the dumplings in his stomach to fishing weights.

Ronny would certainly see his toilet trick as a lie. From talking to her today he knew if he lost her trust, he'd likely never win it back.

How he wished he could take a mulligan. Two deep breaths in and out and he felt telling her now would be better than telling her later, but Jess burst through the door right as the words were perched on his lips.

The smile that graced her face as she took in their hands matched his when he realized Ronny hadn't pulled away yet.

"Well, hello, you two. How's the dryer and the chicken and dumplings? Both good, I hope," Jess inquired as she set her bag down and walked into the kitchen like she wasn't excited.

Once she was behind Ronny she mouthed, "*Oh my god,*" and pointed to their hands like she'd just hit the Lotto. If possible, his smile grew at his friend's excitement.

"Wait," Ronny said, and released him to stand in front of her friend. "You have glasses?"

Clay noticed now too. "Oh, yeah. Sorry, I didn't notice. They look great on you." How he'd missed it was beyond him, but he was sure it was because all he could see was Veronica.

"Yeah, getting old over here. Sit back down and I'll join you. I am starving."

VERONICA

"**I**'d love to stay and chat some more, but I've gotta run. My furniture isn't going to move itself." Clay stood and ran his hand across the back of his neck in the shy way he had. It was very hot. *Wow, that's new.*

"Jess, you look amazing, as always. Veronica, thanks for lunch and the best company I've shared a meal with in a long time."

"Hey," Jess piped up while serving herself a bowl. "I just ate with you a few nights ago, am I chopped liver?" She slid a mischievous look Ronny's way and she caught on. They both turned, folded arms and indignant looks aimed right at Clay before bursting out laughing. He stiffened almost immediately.

"We had dinner, Jess, so not the same thing. But let me make up for my inadvertent insult by inviting you both to a picnic at the dog park. Roscoe would love to introduce you to his friends and I'd love the company."

Ronny may have been out of the real-world loop for a while but Clay didn't even spare Jess a glance, he was only looking at her. That gave her the flutters again, but not enough to brave the public.

"Um, I . . . I'm not really . . . I—"

Ronny stammered until Jess interrupted, "What she's trying to say is we can't make it tomorrow, but maybe in a few days."

"Sure, sure. No problem. Give me a call if your plans change, I'd really like to see you again. I should get going. Don't hesitate to call if you need anything, ladies."

Once he closed the door behind him, they both made their way to the window to watch him leave.

"He is a good-looking man, good heart too," said Jess, and all Ronny could do was nod in agreement. Her attention was completely captivated by the man who was the topic of conversation. One who handled her with kid gloves—not to protect her but to allow her to protect herself.

The way he made her feel was indescribable. What he was teaching her, what he had already taught her was therapeutic. His mom was right, there was something empowering about fixing things.

Ronny could have never opened up to him under other circumstances. She did get a power boost from knowing she could go in there right now and replace that dryer hose by herself.

After Clay got into his truck, he tossed up a hand to them and backed out of the drive. They both stood there and watched until his taillights disappeared into the dusk.

After Clay's truck disappeared, Jess turned so fast Ronny almost landed on her backside as her friend scooped her up and spun her around. All while screaming, "Oh my god, oh my god, oh my god."

Jess's enthusiasm was infectious and Ronny caught it like the flu. Before she knew it, they were dancing around like they used to when the other liked someone.

"Tonight is wine night for sure. How about I run to the store and grab a bottle of pinot and a box of Little Debbie's, and you pick the on demand to watch?"

It was a solid suggestion and plan. "You're on. But maybe we watch a classic action movie instead of my typical choice."

"Wow, what did that man do to you? It's like you're a whole new person. God, I've missed you."

I've missed me too, is what she wanted to say, but instead opted for cautiously optimistic, and said, "I hate to say it, but I'll never be the old me, Jess. That me is gone, changed, but I do see the potential for a better me. Better than yesterday me, I mean."

"Isn't that what we all really are anyway? Works for me."

How did she get so lucky to get not one but two people in her life who got her and helped her find herself?

"I don't know if I ever really thanked you. I mean, yes, I said the words after you got me through a bad night or a rough day. I told you after I leaned on you, but I don't think I ever just . . . told you. Thank you for being you. Not just when you pulled me out of the pit or celebrated with me. But thank you for just sitting here and shoveling dumplings in your mouth and talking about wine."

Jess reached for her hand much as she had Clay's. She curled one finger around one of hers and they sat there while Jess finished her late lunch which was really dinner at that point.

"But in all seriousness, the dryer is fixed, right? Please tell me I didn't mess things up too bad?"

"Yes, the dryer . . ." Her words trailed off and Jess's registered in her sluggish brain. She had to blame the dopamine or whatever hormone flooded higher thinking when you were attracted to someone.

"Jess, what did you mean about the dryer?"

The shoveling hit warp speed and she tried to answer innocently with her mouth full.

"Oh no you don't—swallow and then not another bite until you answer me. What did you mean mess up the dryer?"

"Oh, all right." Jess took her bowl and spoon to the sink and Ronny joined her with the other two and as they rinsed, her friend confessed to her deception.

"After he fixed the door, I saw the way Clay looked at you. I was so obsessed with the fact he didn't want to go out with me back in the day that I couldn't see the fact that I didn't really want to go out with him. But when I saw him look at you, I knew he liked you in a way he was never attracted to me. And you didn't run and hide on your room."

She sighed and deflated. Ronny hated deception but Jess hadn't done anything wrong, right?

"Anyway, when I saw that, the wheels started turning but they didn't go anywhere, just spun in place. I didn't know of a way for the two of you to spend time together. Safe, non-threatening time."

Jess turned and held both her hands. "But after he fixed the toilet, I saw the way you looked at him. Like the way you used to look at men you found attractive. Like we all should at our age. Anyway, I wanted to see that look on your face again, like really wanted to. Not to mention Clay's."

Dropping her hands, she started to pace. Ronny was getting a sinking feeling.

"But when you sat in the living room with confidence, and you put chips on your sandwich and picked out cabinet pulls. I would have done anything to see that again. That spark of confidence. So, I tore the hose on the dryer and pulled it from the wall."

Jess hitched her chin up and crossed her arms. "And I would do it again if what I saw when I walked in can happen. And I won't apologize for it. You were you, not the old you, no, but you. Not just the ghost of the old you haunting this house. If you hate me for it, well, it was worth it."

I can't believe what I just heard. More so, she couldn't believe she wasn't pissed. Deception was wrong, period. But the way she felt wasn't. How could it be. Jess was right, she had been haunting the house.

That was going to stop. It would end and she would live . . . She wasn't ready to go dancing in a bar or even walk through a crowded grocery store parking lot alone, but maybe with Jess or Clay she could do some of those things.

Before her friend could suffer the unknown of Ronny's feelings another minute, she launched herself at her and hugged her tight.

It didn't panic her when she returned the embrace. "So you forgive me then?"

"No, there is nothing to forgive. You helped me and no one was hurt in the process. I think I can learn to accept that intentions matter and deception isn't so black and white."

"I love you, Ronny, and welcome to the gray." For the first time, she didn't think of the gray as such a bad place.

After they recovered from their crying hug fest, Jess grabbed her bag and headed to the store for the provisions. Ronny finished cleaning the kitchen and opened up her laptop. Scrolling through Amazon to see if

Sam JD Hunt had anything new, *Redemption* caught her eye. Hot cover model and a perfect title to dive back into reading. One-click later and it would be here in less than forty-eight hours.

She'd let Jess hold on to *Taken* and her copy of *Torn*, and she'd get to dive into *Redemption*.

A quick scan of the people who *bought this also*, netted her a "to be read" list that was shaping up to sound naughty.

After closing the screen and donning her pjs, Jess still wasn't back and Ronny started thinking. She did want to spend some more time with Clay, but she wasn't really ready to go on a date yet. How could she see him again?

No. No, no, no, no, no. You are not even thinking it.

But she was. Before she could chicken out, she grabbed the bag of potatoes from the pantry, then turned on the garbage disposal. She fed the monster carbs until it just hummed and nothing else happened.

She looked at the bag which only had two potatoes left. She basically carb loaded the disposal.

Jess's headlights bounced off the window as she pulled into the shed. Ronny rushed to clean up the crime scene and remove the evidence. She felt bad . . . well, kind of bad.

CLAYTON

"**S**o, what's with you today?" Charlie stopped with the fencing to wipe his brow . . . and give Clay a hard time.

"You're literally the hardest working man I know, yet you're letting me do this fence practically by myself. You're just standing there with a goofy ass grin on your face."

"Now, you watch that mouth of yours, Mr. Thompson. You'll not get a lady's attention with that kind of language." Mrs. Wilson scolded Charlie while she served them water and apples.

Keeping a straight face was almost too much for him as Charlie stumbled over an apology. Mrs. Wilson was probably the most foul-mouthed old church lady he knew. Of course, most folks didn't hear that side of her.

She'd driven a school bus for thirty-five years. Kept a clean vocabulary through every route she'd ever driven. When they force retired her and she didn't have the kids anymore, her language went to hell in a handbasket, so to speak.

Oh, she still played the part of sweet little old lady well, but Clay knew better.

Rather than sell her out to Charlie since she was actually being nice to him, Clay bit into his apple and shut his mouth.

She hopped up on the tailgate of Clay's truck and surveyed their work while they drank and snacked. "You weren't lying when you said you could do it in a couple of days, were you?"

"No, ma'am. We should be finished up this afternoon and Thomas and Agnes can get to courting." At his pronouncement, Mrs. Wilson bobbed her head once and hopped down from the tailgate like someone half her age.

She gave Charlie a quick pat on the back as she passed, shocking them both, but not as much as the words that came from her mouth next. "You mean fucking, Clayton. Plain and simple."

His finger flew to his ear and gave it a quick shake to clean it out. Sure, she had a vocabulary, but he'd never heard her drop an f-bomb before.

"Oh crap, did she really just say that? She's got a mouth on her."

"I told you she did, Charlie, you just didn't believe me. Let's finish this up, I want to get the rest of my stuff moved into the house."

"Even more shocking," Charlie rambled as he got to work. "I think she likes me more than you now. You see how she patted me on the back. She didn't pat you. Yep, I won her over with my sparkling personality and irresistible charm."

Clay shook his head and let Charlie enjoy his hard-won victory. If Mrs. Wilson accepted him, the whole town would. She was the key to living in Bellwood. Clay suspected she'd been here when the colonies were formed. He laughed at his own silent joke.

Yep, I'm certifiable. Telling myself jokes and laughing at them too.

"Right, your charm, and how many ladies not in AARP has that won over for you?"

"Ha," Charlie barked a laugh. "I do just fine with the younger crowd, don't you worry. Wait, that didn't come out right."

Before Charlie could dig the hole deeper, Clay was laughing so hard his side hurt. "You sound like a perv right now, you know that right?"

"Yeah, it came out all wrong, but at least I'm not hung up on someone who won't even go out with me."

Clay's laughter died immediately.

"Sorry, Clay. I didn't mean it like that, I was just giving you a hard time."

Charlie was a genuinely nice person and Clay knew he didn't really mean anything by it, but it stung all the same.

A sense of despair washed over him. What if Ronny was never ready to be in any kind of intimate relationship? Could he cut his losses and find a woman who could be his partner in all aspects of life?

"Dang it," he muttered under his breath. That was exactly why he didn't date women like Ronny. Not that he felt her inferior in any way, she was better than him hands down. Clay had just built this life plan and Ronny was trying to toss it in the trash.

Charlie finished up the fencing and was cleaning up while Clay had been working by muscle memory while lost in thought. He hadn't even realized how much time had passed.

"Clay, you know earlier . . . I didn't mean it the way it sounded. I didn't mean any insult by it, I was just ribbing. I hope you know that. I would never say a negative word about Jess or Veronica. I can see how bad you got it for that girl. I can also see how your friendship has grown with Jess. They make you a better man, I would never bag on that."

He clapped him on the shoulder once and started loading the truck. Charlie and he had always talked about stuff, even feelings, so he shouldn't feel out of place continuing the conversation, but he did.

Needing to know though trumped comfort. "What do you mean I've got it bad and I'm better. I haven't really talked about them that much, have I?"

Charlie turned and pinned him with a serious gaze. "No, you haven't and that's one of the ways I know. You've always protected the people you care about the most. Privacy. When you ramble on about someone, I know it won't last. Like Rebecca from the store. After you asked her out, you wouldn't shut up about it."

Loading more fence scraps onto the truck, he continued, "I wasn't surprised when you didn't even make it to the first date. Then there was the Food Bear girl, what's her name. Worst date ever but you were cheerful and optimistic for the second date that never happened. Should I go on?"

Clay joined him in cleaning up the scraps. "No, I think you made your point. But I don't know what to do about Ronny. She's amazing. She's funny, and thoughtful, of course, beautiful, but I have a plan and she may not ever fit into my timeline."

"Jesus, you and that infernal plan. Plans change, man, especially if there's someone worth changing them for. So your timeline is off, boo-hoo. Do you care enough about her to see where it can lead? That's not even a real question. I can tell you care more than I've seen you care about anyone else. The real question is can you let go of your life plan to make room for her?"

God, he hated and loved Charlie right now so much. He had a way of getting to the heart of the matter. Charlie wasn't a well-spoken man, used as few words as possible, but when he spoke, what he said mattered.

It was hard to let go of something when you've clung to it for so long. His plan wasn't just a plan, it had been a blueprint for his life. If he didn't follow it he would be living day to day, flying by the seat of his pants.

But wasn't Ronny worth it? Wasn't he trying to get her to do the same thing? Let go of the guiding force in her life and live each moment as it came. Let go.

Realization was like a blow to the head. That was exactly what it was. He was asking her to let go and he wouldn't. *What if I don't let go? I'll always wonder what if.*

"You know what, Charlie, you're a wise man."

"Don't you want to know how you're better?" Clay could tell by the look in Charlie's eye he wasn't going to get the real answer. Not now anyway.

"Okay, I'll bite, how am I better?" He fired up the truck and they headed back to the shop.

"Better because you're going to buy me dinner at Rusty's for doing a bang-up job and making Mrs. Wilson fall in love with me."

Laughter filled the truck and Clay enjoyed the lighter mood that enveloped him at letting go. It was scary to be without his life plan for the first time in his adult life. But there was freedom in the fear.

VERONICA

Ugh, use the dang disposal already. It had been almost two whole days and Jess had managed not to use the garbage disposal.

Ronny was about ready to just march up to the sink and flip the switch herself, but it would be too obvious. Jess had cleared all their plates and scraped them in the trash.

There was no way she was letting Jess even suspect she'd staged it so Clay would come over and teach her more. She would never live it down.

But if Jess kept scraping everything in the trash, she'd never see Clay again or learn how to fix the disposal.

As much as she wanted to see Clay, and she did, she needed to learn to fix the dang disposal too.

He'd been right, or rather his mom had been. She was feeling very Rosie Riveter lately. There was real power in it. Not in a way she could elegantly explain, not even to herself.

For whatever reason, the mailman had held her box of books at the post office instead of dropping it on the porch as usual. Earlier that day, she'd shocked herself when she'd jumped in the passenger seat as Jess headed out to grab it.

She hadn't gotten out of the car, she let Jess claim the box. But she had sat in the parking lot with the window half down while people milled about with their mail and packages. She even smiled at some.

It must have come off more like a scowl because it hadn't been returned. But inexplicably, she was okay with that.

"Oh, forget it." If she wanted it done right, she was going to have to do it herself. *Thanks for nothing, Jess. Now, what to use.* She couldn't just walk over and flip the switch, she needed something to dispose of.

Rummaging through the refrigerator she found a wilted bowl of salad and some left-over spaghetti from last week. "Perfect."

"Ew, you aren't going to eat that are you? That needs to be tossed. If you're hungry, I can make us something because I could eat."

Jess snatched the Tupperware off the counter and headed toward the trash. "Don't do that, it'll stink, put it down the sink."

"Good call," Jess responded as she dumped the salad, turned on the faucet, and flipped the switch to grind up the limp lettuce.

Nothing happened, just a whirring sound. Jess flipped the switch again and again with the same result. "Ugh." She tipped her head back and reached for her phone. Ronny turned her attention to the vegetable crisper like it was the most interesting thing in the world.

Containing her excitement was almost impossible as she listened in to one side of the conversation.

She filled in the other side in her mind with Clay's husky voice. He always sounded like he was on the verge of a cough.

"Yeah, it just makes a whirring sound and nothing else."

"No clanking racket? Did you put anything in it?"

"No, I haven't even touched it for a few days."

"Okay, I'll be right over and tell Ronny I said hi."

"Thanks, you're the best."

When Jess ended the call, Ronny turned her attention to an imaginary speck on the counter, scraping at it with her fingernail.

"So?" Even she could hear she'd failed to keep the excitement out of her voice.

"Sooooo, eager beaver, he'll be here within the hour with a new disposal." The intensity Jess was studying her with made her uncomfortable.

"Why are you looking at me like that?"

"I don't know yet, I'll let you know when I do." Jess cleared the sink as best she could and took the salad and spaghetti to the trash.

"Oh, I could really use a hot bath. You good if I leave the door open and Clay can let himself in or you can?"

"Yes. Yes, leave the door open and I'll wait here at the table."

That answer stunned her as much as it did Jess. Jess being Jess, had a big old grin on her face and hugged her tight. She didn't pick or tease, more than normal. A small, "get it, girl" and she was gone.

Ronny plopped down at the table to wait. She wasn't good at flirting. What was she thinking? She should just run to her nest, leave a note for Clay and be done.

And she most certainly wasn't good at deception. She cut her glance to the sink. In her imagination, she saw potatoes shooting up from the drain in a fountain and dancing across the countertop.

Just as they started a tap routine, complete with top hats and a liar song, there was a banging on the screen door. It pulled her from the potato chorus line that was taunting her.

Come in was poised on her lips, but she took a deep breath and stood instead. Before she could talk herself out of it, she practically ran to the door and threw open the screen.

Clay stepped back to avoid being whacked with it.

"Sorry," she apologized sheepishly. Instead of coming in, Clay just stood there. Hands full with a box she assumed contained a new disposal.

Thank goodness he didn't have a toolbox today or he might have ended up on his backside when he jumped back from the swinging screen door.

Ronny used her free hand to wave him past her. This was a test for her, one she was going to pass come hell or high water. The look on his handsome face made her think it was a test for him too.

After a stand-off that lasted just a few seconds but felt longer, Clay nodded and scooted around her. Once he was past and headed to the kitchen, she let out the breath she was holding to fortify her.

But it was drowned out by him. Something about him recognizing the moment as pivotal made it even more so.

Leaving the door open to enjoy the crisp pine scented breeze, she followed him into the kitchen. Clay had set the box on the table and turned to face her.

Wow, he looked blue collar hot in flannel and a toolbelt. He should forsake the toolbox more often.

Nerves were wreaking havoc on her vocabulary and thought process. "Garbage thingamajig," she pointed. "There."

"Yeah, that's where they usually are."

Right, like I keep it somewhere else. I'm such an idiot.
Wringing her hands, she dropped her gaze to her feet.

First, she saw the toes of his boots then his hand reaching for hers. She didn't protest when he encouraged them apart by linking his pinkie to hers.

"Hey, I was just kidding." Ugh, he was making it worse. He thought she was embarrassed because of her idiotic statement. She was embarrassed because she wanted to kiss him, wanted him to kiss her.

The thought hit her hard. Ronny never expected to be attracted to a man in that way ever again. She'd thought that was just another thing stolen from her, but it wasn't. Sure, she'd misplaced it for a while, but it was back.

When she first started having those thoughts she'd lean against the toilet for hours, waiting for the nausea to roll in and remind her she was broken.

But it never came. The thought of being intimate with Clay didn't feel at all like she expected.

While she was feeding the garbage disposal an overabundance of starch, she realized why . . . she was falling for him.

A healthy dose of doubt came speeding in on the bumper of that thought. He was the first man she'd spent time with. The first man allowed in her home and the first man who didn't feel like a threat.

Was that why? Did it have anything to do with him as a man at all? She hated the self-doubt, but she needed to spend time with him and see. She also needed to spend time out, with other people too.

Ronny had to know if it was Clayton Briggs who sent the butterflies in her stomach into a frenzy or if it was just because she spent less than zero time with other people.

As much as her heart said it was him with his quiet wisdom, crooked smile, and quirky humor, her head told her to be sure.

Right now, his touch was warming her chest. The heat tracked up her pinkie finger, through her arm and exploded like Independence Day fireworks in her heart.

"I'm not embarrassed. I mean, I am, but not by that. I mean . . ." Deep breath in, cleansing breath out. "Do you want to have dinner sometime?"

It was a mistake to look up. Clay was smiling with his whole face, heck, his whole body. It was, breathtaking. "Are you asking me on a date, Ronny."

He called her Ronny for the first time. It seemed more familiar than Veronica.

"Yes . . . but I'll probably bring Jess along. Is that okay?"

Clay took her other pinkie in his and swung their hands like she remembered doing in grade school.

"Any time spent with you is more than okay." Clay squeezed her fingers and stared into her eyes. "Well, I should get to work."

The words said one thing, but his eyes and reluctance to let go said another. Ronny hated to break the spell, but she was sure if she didn't let go, they would stand here for a lifetime. She felt the loss keenly the millisecond she reached for the box and let him go.

Studying the brand and description like she knew anything about it. She felt another brick of guilt tossed on the pile at the money he'd spent because of her. Why couldn't she just be normal and ask him out without the ruse.

CLAYTON

Letting go wasn't possible. Clay wanted to stand there all night, but the intensity clearly got to Ronny.

Something was off about her tonight but maybe it was just . . . "Where's Jess? Should I come back or . . . ?" He figured he looked like a cornered animal looking for an escape.

"Oh . . . um, no. I'm fine, just I'm excited to learn the inner workings of this puppy here." Her hand landed on the box. "Or, not so inner. How can you be sure it can't be repaired?"

"Actually, I'm not. But I'm also not an expert at repairing one of these. Besides, I am assuming the one you have is probably old unless your grandmother had it replaced. But either way, you'll learn a lot."

He wasn't thrilled with the twinge of disappointment he saw in her captivating eyes. But as soon as he started explaining the first steps of turning off water and power, it disappeared.

Replaced with a sparkle he wanted to see there all the time.

As he crawled under the sink and turned on his back, Ronny shuffled closer and sat cross-legged by his knees.

Somehow that felt significant to him. Even when they held fingers, she could bolt at any time. But, the way she was sitting, she would be vulnerable if he meant her harm. To him that translated to trust.

Stopping the smile in his heart was beyond impossible. That simple act meant more than almost anything she could have done.

She trusts me.

Clay would sooner die than to toss that precious gift away.

"Ronny, would you mind grabbing the flashlight and holding it here for me? It'll be easier for you to see too."

When she reached for the flashlight on his toolbelt he froze. He half expected her to use the light from her phone instead.

This Ronny was so different than the one he'd spied through the window. Even from the one he'd shared chicken and dumplings with a few days ago.

"You can't really see back here, but you need to loosen this." He heard scraping and rustling beside him and then her head appeared and disappeared.

When she slid in on her back beside him, separated only by the cabinet bar, he thought he was imagining it.

Maybe he'd startled when she reached for the flashlight and conked his head against the disposal and this was a dream. It was a tight fit so definitely a possibility.

The light hit the exact spot he was working on and her scent invaded his senses. Wildflowers and fresh grass. Spring, she smelled like spring when everything was new.

Averting his eyes from the task at hand because he wanted—no needed—to see her this close. She was so close that the flyaway red strands of her hair tickled his cheek. Her eyes were glued to where he was loosening the connection. Up this close, her eyes were even more stunning. Clay had never seen that color before, not without contacts.

"Clay?" Her tone said that wasn't the first time she'd called his name. Instead of continuing his appraisal of her through a sideways glance, he turned his head toward her heart shaped face.

Her pink bow shaped lips mesmerized him. Watching them form his name was scrambling his brain.

"Clay?"

"Yeah?"

"There's goopy gunk dripping on your chest."

All he could think about was kissing her. Tasting those lips and feeding his soul with the mewls he imagined she might make as he did so.

"I don't care, can I kiss you?"

"What?" It was a breathy stunned response that took his control to its limit. She didn't seem repelled by the idea.

"Please? If I don't . . ." His plea died on his tongue when hers darted out and swept across her full lower lip.

She nodded slightly and he awkwardly used the only arm he could maneuver her way in the cramped space to bring her face closer to his.

There was a moment of hesitation on his part, he wanted to be beyond certain he not only had permission but that she wanted it as much as he did.

The answer he needed was there in every angle of her face and facet of her eyes. When his lips met hers, he felt immortal.

Clay was a goner. Not only did he know it, he relished it. He was invincible to every other force on earth except her.

She would be able to slay him with her tears and redeem him with her smile. He was so far off his game and lost in her that he didn't deepen the kiss. Just stayed there pressing small smacking kisses and then a lingering one against her lips.

When he felt her tongue poke shyly at his lips, he realized he had all the finesse of a fifteen-year-old.

Taking her cue, he shifted to turn the innocent first kiss to something more.

Their lips separated when his shoulder hit the garbage disposal and a glop of something foul smelling plopped down and killed the mood.

They both found it funnier than anything. She was breathing heavy and her lips looked glossy but it was her eyes that caught his attention.

Not even the foul-smelling glops plopping down on him could overshadow what he saw there—or rather what he didn't see—the haunted look was gone.

"Let me shimmy this loose and I'll let you install the new one," Clay said to get them back on task and away from their kiss. Ronny's cheeks heated as she nodded and slipped out from under the sink.

He made quick work of removing the disposal now that the majority of any lingering grossness was all over him.

Standing, he turned and set the disposal in the other sink and removed his disgusting shirt before he gagged and totally lost all manliness.

The ego boost of a lifetime awaited him as he turned back toward the table to grab the new disposal.

Ronny stood there, new disposal in hand, with jaw on the floor and eyes bugging out of her head. It was almost comical. He expected a cartoon "Zoinks!" sound and heart eyes to pop off her face.

Clay couldn't help himself and he flexed his pecs in such a way that Terry Crews would have high-fived him.

Cloud nine wasn't high enough to describe how he felt. He was again invincible because of her.

When she cleared her throat and averted her eyes, he was torn between thumping his chest like a maniac and crippling insecurity.

"Um, sorry about your shirt." She was staring at her toes. A move that broke his heart when it was because she was insecure, but one that repaired it when it was because she was so obviously flustered by him.

"No worries, I have a spare in the truck, but let's get this puppy in and get you chewing up leftovers in no time."

"Okay."

"Here, take this." Clay handed her his wrench. "Now, I'll hold up the housing and you connect it there and there"—Clay pointed to the two holes he described—"Tighten both but don't over tighten. We just need it to form a tight seal for those"—Clay again pointed out what he was referencing— "Up there, those hold up the weight so make sure they are snug enough."

Holding the flashlight with his mouth, he directed the beam where it was needed. Ronny did as instructed with a massive smile on her face.

He spat the flashlight out so he could speak. "Okay, slide out from under it so if there's an issue, it doesn't come down on top of you."

It was all clapping and cheering when he let go and it stayed in place. "Good job, Ronny." She sat cross-legged examining the repair when he slid out from under the sink.

Captivated by her radiance, he leaned against the cabinet and just absorbed her pride and joy at her work.

Jess joined them. She took in his appearance. One knee on the ground, one up with his elbow on it, no shirt, and staring at Ronny like a lovestruck puppy. Jess seemed initially confused but she recovered quickly.

"Is it done?"

"Almost," he answered as he stood. "We just need to turn everything back on and give it a test run."

VERONICA

"**G**reat job, you two. Color me impressed." As much as Clay's compliments did for her, impressing Jess seemed bigger somehow.

Jess was with her every step of the way and celebrated milestones with her but this was different. She was *proud* and not of something Ronny finally overcame but something she did. Something she decided she wanted to do and did. Not something that everyone her age already did but she'd lost because of what happened to her.

It was simply different for some reason and she loved it. Of course, Clay's chest was distracting her from almost everything else. His jeans hung low and he had that V that made girls stupid, including her.

"I'll just take this to the truck and grab a clean shirt, then come back in and tidy up a bit."

Jess had the same look on her face as she imagined she did and they both nodded like twins. A half smile crept onto Clay's face as he passed, his gaze firmly on her and her alone.

After he passed, she enjoyed watching him walk toward the front door. His back was cut but lean, and he had that faint diamond shape in the middle. The way his butt looked in those faded jeans made her weak in the knees.

So lost in watching him walk away, she missed Jess staring at her and catching flies. It wasn't until she pinched her biceps that she averted her gaze as he exited the house.

The look on Jess's face was downright comical. Her eyes were swimming with joy or something. "Oh my god, you were totally eye humping him." Her friend paused and glanced back to make sure he was outside. "You . . . wow, when you find your groove, Stella, you really find your groove."

"We kissed." She just blurted it out. No preamble, nothing, just two words shot from her mouth like a Colt 45.

If she thought Jess's expression was comical before, now her friend looked so laughable, she couldn't help herself. She devolved into breath robbing laughter.

Jess joined her and before long there were tears streaming down her face. "I hear lover boy climbing the stairs so I'm going to make myself scarce." She made smooching sounds as she bounced down the hall.

Clay opened the screen door and almost ran into Jess. Lost in reliving the kiss, she almost missed Jess lean up and whisper something in Clay's ear. They shared a friendly embrace and Jess winked at her before she headed to her wing of the house.

The way Clay approached reminded her of the slow seductive way a dancer took the stage. The plain white tee was almost more attractive than his shirtless look . . . almost.

The need to share more about her past to him was overwhelming in more ways than one. She'd never shown anyone but Jess her nest. Better he see it now than after her whole heart was in his hands.

If he can handle the nest, I can trust him with more.
"I want to show you something, but . . ." She let her words die, she had a harder time asking him to not judge her than she expected.

"Hey." Clay reached for her hand, but instead of stopping at just one finger, he curled his strong fingers around three. "You can show me anything."

"Okay, but please don't think I'm crazy." She led him to her door. "I don't think I can handle it if you do."

With a deep inhale, she held it in and opened the door to what had been her sanctuary for almost a year.

She shifted to the side to make a path for him to enter. When he stepped into her room, the breath she'd been holding whooshed from her lungs with the force of a hurricane.

When her breath quickened, her hand flew to her stomach. The room was getting wobbly. All because she was terrified of what he would think about her space, not about him being in her room.

A soft touch landed atop her hand on her stomach. Gently, Clay pried it away and brushed his lips across the knuckles. When he let their hands dangle between them, he didn't completely let go, he kept her hand in his and interlaced their fingers.

The palm to palm contact helped her focus. His very presence fortified her. "This is where I sleep." The words were easy compared to pointing to the nest in the corner rather than the bed on the other side of the window.

It was hard, but she pulled her focus to his face, she needed to see his reaction even if it ripped her to shreds.

The moment his face turned to the nest, she squeezed his hand harder. Maybe for support or maybe to relay the importance, she wasn't sure which.

His features gave nothing away. His voice however, was thick with emotion. "Is it safety for you?"

"Yes. I just couldn't sleep in a bed. I know it's silly but—"

"Ronny, nothing that makes you feel safe is silly." Using their connected hands, Clay pulled her into an embrace. Their first real embrace, in her bedroom . . . no escape.

Instead of panicking, she melted into his body and drenched his shirt with tears. "I've just always thought if someone came in, they'd look for me on the bed and I'd be able to get away or fight back or shoot them."

He dropped a kiss on the side of her head. "Not silly at all. It sounds like you found survival tactics."

That's exactly what she'd done. He was the first person who didn't look concerned when they learned of one of her tactics, including her therapists. Even if they never worked, in her mind they would and that's what mattered.

"When I was attacked, it was just . . . I . . ." *Just say something, Ronny, anything.* "It was more robbery to me. The word fits better than rape."

There, she said the word and didn't burst into flames. And with that spoken word the bar to her mental prison just disintegrated.

"He stole from my body, my mind, my past, and my future. He stole my love of design, music, dancing, you name it. He stole more than anyone can imagine. I couldn't stop him from doing what he did, it took me a long time to come to terms with that."

The arms wrapped around her shifted and felt all encompassing. *Safe.* Something about Clay was a healing balm on old wounds, but it wasn't all him. It was her. She was stitching together internal gashes that had been seeping and slowly killing her.

She was powerful now, she could replace a garbage disposal and kiss a man and fix a toilet that won't flush and tell her story.

"It wasn't my fault just because I had been drinking. It wasn't my fault he was obsessed with me and my short skirts and high heels. But what *was* my fault, was not accepting that a long time ago, and for letting him continue to rob from me even though he's dead."

"Honey, not even that is your fault. You needed time to heal and find yourself. You are amazing. Some people never find their way back."

"Yeah, but I spent a lot of time looking for the old me and she's gone." Shamelessly, she rubbed her face against the shoulder of his shirt to dry some of the tears.

It was then he did the most unexpected thing. Clay released her with one hand, putting some distance between them and lifted his shirt. He gently cleaned her face with it.

"That day when you showed us how to fix a toilet, I wished so hard that you could have known the old me. I thought she was someone you could fall for. But then when I learned how to fix a dryer, I realized I can embrace a new me, because old me would have never done something like that."

Being this open was draining, but there was one other thing she was compelled to show him. "Or that."

She pointed to her mussed twin bed across the room.

Waiting for him to understand was too much, she couldn't bear the wait. "The day we fixed the dryer, I went to sleep in my nest like every other night, but when I got up to go to the bathroom, I must've climbed in there. I woke up the next morning and was confused where I was."

Her voice was barely audible and scratchy from crying. Her eyes kept trying to close, she was exhausted.

Clay pulled her into his hard chest so fast it made her dizzy. "Thank you for sharing that with me. I know it wasn't easy and I feel honored you chose to let me in. I won't let you down. And for the record nothing you say will scare me off."

Cherished. That was what she felt. Never in the history of her relationships had she felt cherished. They didn't even have a traditional relationship . . . not yet. But she felt more for him in a short time than she did for her longest relationship of three years.

When he kissed her temple again it was all she could do not to blurt out words of love or undying devotion. Thank god another yawn kept her from doing that. She still didn't know how to approach the whole asking him out thing. So telling him she had feelings was certainly off the table. What man wanted a woman like her to fall for him so quickly.

"I should go and let you get some sleep. You seem tired. Come and lock up behind me so you can get some rest."

CLAYTON

If he'd had the ability to lock the deadbolt from outside, he would have tucked Ronny into her bed last night.

It had been downright overwhelming him to do so. But her safety won out over his need. The drive home had passed in a blur and he counted himself lucky he'd made it.

His trailer felt empty when he'd arrived, lonely. Most of his stuff was in the house waiting for him to spend his first night there.

After the night of firsts he'd shared with Ronny, he decided not to spend his first night in his house just yet. Alone. Instead, he'd pulled the linens still left in the trailer down and made a pallet on the floor. A nest.

He'd had a fitful night's sleep on the unforgiving floor but had woken up in the best mood he'd been in for a long time.

No jobs were scheduled so he decided clearing out the trailer was on the agenda.

The sooner it was empty, the sooner he could be rid of that part of his existence. There was so much symbolism in his life right now he couldn't even fathom it all.

New beginnings, shedding the past. Even Mrs. Wilson was a symbol. An example of how to let go of preconceived notions and see what's right in front of his face.

"Please tell me you made coffee?" Charlie entering the office rocked him back. He'd been sitting at his desk doing some bookkeeping that desperately needed done and of course thinking about symbols and Ronny and Mrs. Wilson and her goats, he'd totally tuned out the ding that alerted him to the door opening.

"Shoot, you scared the crap out of me."

Charlie poured them both cups of coffee and joined him at the desk catty corner to his.

"I've been doing that a lot lately. You've got your mind on Veronica and looking moon-eyed and lost."

Clay couldn't deny Charlie's claim, and he didn't want to. He'd fallen hard for a woman he'd only known a short time and that didn't bother him as expected. The part that did though was wondering if she felt the same way and could she move at his pace? He'd wait if she couldn't, but he genuinely hoped she could.

"How long do you think you have to know someone to really know if they're the one for you?"

"Do you mean like a standard time? There is no set time. Do you really want to know what I think about the matter or are you just talking it through out loud?"

"I asked you, didn't I?" Clay refilled his coffee and sat back down, pushing the books aside and propping up his feet.

Talking about feelings may not be normal for a lot of men, but it was for him. It was how he was raised so it came naturally. Charlie was a little different and Clay learned a while back that the more manly stance he took, the more emotion and honesty he could pull from Charlie. If it got too girly, Charlie would start joking and cracking wise.

"Well, I don't think time is a factor. I believe knowing someone—really knowing them—is. Not like what their favorite color is, you can know that about a practical stranger. Things like that ain't got squat to do with how *well* you know someone. That depends on how that time together was spent."

Charlie could have jumped up and started reciting Shakespeare in the Queen's English and Clay still wouldn't have been as surprised as he was at his words.

"Well, I know how she sleeps because it makes her feel safe. I know that she wants to turn her grandmother's house into a design showroom but hasn't yet. And I know that when she's happy with herself she tilts her head to the left and sets her jaw."

A picture of the way her freckles squished together when she laughed popped into his mind. Along with a million other images, like how she buried her nose in Roscoe's neck when insecurity crept into her eyes or how she turned to Jess for intervention when things were too much for her. Or how her voice got stronger and weaker at the same time when she talked about her Gram.

"And what's her favorite color?"

"Not a clue."

Charlie dropped his feet to the ground and shuffled papers around his desk. Clay could tell it was getting a little heavy for him. He didn't like to talk about his last relationship. Oh, he'd rattle on about all the others and even imaginary future ones, but Leslie was off limits.

There was a story there, but Clay tried not to pry, not when that subject was Fort Knox. Clay had spent time with them on multiple occasions and still didn't have a clue what happened. He suspected his feelings for Ronny were hitting too close to home for Charlie.

"Then, my friend, I'd say you are long gone. Might as well buy a ring and pop the question at this point. But favorite color might be important when decorating, so just this once, I say ask the question."

While there was sadness in his friend's voice, there was happiness too. Charlie had given him a lot to think about.

Diving into the deep end headfirst when he wanted something was the way Clay operated . . . after checking the depth. He'd decided to drop out of college and open a construction business after only considering it for two days. Of course, during those two days he'd written a full business plan and projections for a decade. So while he did make quick decisions and stick with them, he didn't go all in blind.

"What do you say, we go over to Egg Hut and grab some pancakes? Then I'll pay you extra to help me empty out the trailer and get everything into the house. Not much left, just some minor things." It was only fair since Charlie got paid extra for jobs he did for clients.

"Deal, but I'm buying this time. Not only do you need to furnish the new place, it sounds like you might be buying a ring in the near future."

"Deal." Clay checked his phone one more time before they hopped into the truck and three times while they waited on their late breakfast.

"So, I was thinking, since Mrs. Wilson is single now and knows her way around a goat, I might take her to the homecoming dance. What do you think?"

Clay wasn't paying attention, he heard Charlie's voice but his words didn't register. "Sure, why not."

A smack to the back of his skull and roaring laughter pulled him out of his head. Mrs. Wilson, who'd just assaulted him, scooched him over and sat down while Charlie continued laughing.

VERLENE LANDON

"What's so funny?" Clay wasn't enjoying being the butt of their joke but even more so, he seriously wasn't enjoying the fact that Ronny hadn't called him. Sure, it was only eleven thirty, but that didn't make it better.

"Dude, you just gave me permission to take Mrs. Wilson to the school dance."

"Yep and agreed that my finer points are goats."

That was downright funny, so he joined them in merriment. "Sorry, but I was hoping to hear from Ronny and well . . . just forget it, I sound like a wuss."

Another smack landed on the back of his head. "Ouch." He rubbed away the sting. Mrs. Wilson packed a wallop. "Why are you hitting me? You like me, remember? Hit Charlie, he's the bad one."

Getting hit hurt, so he didn't feel one ounce of remorse for selling out his friend. "Oh, please, he's my new favorite." She winked conspiratorially. "So, what has your boxers in a twist?"

He was so not talking to Mrs. Wilson about Ronny. It already felt weird all the way around. First, he spilled to Charlie and he'd practically told him to propose. Then he turned into a marshmallow and gave serious thought to spending his life with her after one freaking kiss.

Time to regroup and assess my feelings. That's what he needed, not a pervy old goat lady and an ex best friend.

It was time to take back his man card, but the fact that Ronny hadn't contacted . . . "Wait, she doesn't have

198

my number. Jess does, but Ronny wouldn't want my number like that, she'd want me to give it to her."

He'd almost added how he was worried she wasn't feeling what he was just feeling too. However, the epic quest to retrieve his man card couldn't begin like that.

"Ha," Mrs. Wilson barked a laugh. "Is that what has your huevos all tangled? Well, sounds like you got it bad."

Before she could continue her ribbing, Charlie joined in. "Clay and Veronica sitting—"

The tiny woman stopped Charlie's grade school song with a wrinkled hand to the air and a look that could wither Mr. Olympia himself.

"Veronica Allen? That's who you're all gooey-eyed over?"

Clay didn't consider himself gooey-eyed, but he nodded anyway. He wasn't about to split hairs with Mrs. Wilson.

She reached below the table and pinched his knee like she was angry, but her eyes told a whole different story. "Sophia was my best friend, and that girl meant the world to her, which translates to the same for me. I've left her to her own after she moved back, waiting for her to . . . Never mind."

She didn't add that she knew why she'd moved back, but it was beyond clear she did. "You hurt her, and I will end you."

The last four words were spoken with such conviction, lord knows he believed her. The relief he felt when she let his skin go was nothing compared to her parting words.

"However, I think you're just what she needs, and vice versa. It's perfect and I approve, and so would Sophia. Make that girl happy and you will have my undying love."

All he could do was stare in stunned silence as she left the diner. It seemed as if everything was telling him they were meant to be. Was he ready to go against what some would call fate?

VERONICA

Clay hadn't called her yet. She kind of expected he was the type who'd text "good morning" just to start her day right.

That worry lasted through brushing her teeth before she realized they didn't exchange information. He had Jess's contact information and she had his, but Ronny didn't.

Jess had offered her his number over breakfast and lunch multiple times, and while she entered it into her phone finally, she still wasn't ready to just call him.

It felt weird and wrong. He hadn't given her his number. Not that she believed he was the type to get angry about it, it still felt like overstepping. People should have a choice in who they give their number to.

And as much as she wanted to have expectations, it wasn't fair to. Sure, she'd already accepted the fact she'd lost her heart to him, but men didn't move that fast. Plus, she felt like she'd pushed the boundaries of deception with her garbage disposal trick.

So, here I sit overthinking things instead of just calling him. Ronny threw herself back on her bed and gave a frustrated cry to the empty room.

Even through the frustration, she got butterflies thinking about Clay and how they'd kissed, and how she wanted more . . . was ready for more.

She rolled her head to the side and took in the folded pile of bedding in the corner. Not a nest, but a neat stack of bedding. She wasn't ready to put it away in the linen closet quite yet. She wanted to keep it close, not just as comfort but as a reminder of the changes in her life.

It defied all reason, but she was in love with Clayton Briggs. Logically, she knew she should take it slow, she was sure her therapist would say the same. But she'd been taking life slow for almost a year. Even before that, she hemmed and hawed about moving back and starting her own business when it was what she wanted. Instead, she convinced herself she was happy in the city, in her job where she'd never get to design on her own.

Even after the attack, she took her recovery slow. Maybe if she'd approached it head-on she could have found herself sooner. She was not going to let Clay slip away because she was overly cautious. What had that gotten her in the past? Nothing good or nothing she wanted, that was for sure. So why was she not going for it with Clay?

When he'd left last night, she hadn't even bothered showering, and fell straight into bed after locking up.

Bed.

Not a nest in the corner, but her bed. Slept there all night long. First thing that morning, she folded her nest. There was a great sense of power and healing that flowed through her.

No one was around but she blushed when she thought about how she'd touched herself in the shower that morning thinking about Clay.

It was the first time she'd done that in a really long time. She could barely believe her body could feel that kind of pleasure anymore.

After the realization about the lack of shared phone numbers smacked her in the face, she thought about loosening a pipe or unscrewing the showerhead. Any excuse to get Clay to come over. But again, that guilt of deception ate away at her.

Besides, everything she could think of breaking, she felt fairly confident she could fix. She wanted a repeat of shower time, but this time with Clay.

And that thought brings me no fear.

The wait was killing her. If she didn't call him, would he call Jess and ask for her? She honestly didn't know so she sat up, took a deep breath and hit the call button.

Before it connected, there was a knock at the door. She aggressively tapped the end button with her fingertip repeatedly and jumped to the window.

Clay's truck.

How did he pull up without her even hearing? *Because you were having dirty thoughts and thinking about touching him.* The way she scolded herself was her least favorite part of New Ronny.

Without overthought or analyzing the situation, Ronny power walked through the kitchen to open the door. When she laid eyes on him, her heart took over and she threw herself into his arms and kissed him.

She gave no thought to invading his personal space, or if he wanted to kiss her or not. She just lived in the moment. If he didn't want it, he'd let her know.

But he did, boy did he. Clay's lips were borderline aggressive, but in a good way, his hands exploring. She felt it when he left the present, and it disappointed her more than it should have.

"Are you okay with this?" His question was beautiful and thoughtful and a million other things, but it was also heartbreaking.

Peeling herself away from him, she picked at her nails. The braver Ronny thought it was time to address the elephant in the room, or rather on the porch. The wounded Ronny wanted to pull into herself and never mention it again.

Thank goodness bravery won over retreat.

"Yes, it was fine. I mean, I thought it was obvious it was fine when I . . . never mind. Will it always be like this for us? I mean assuming there is an us. I just—" She was rambling hard and when her gaze dropped to her feet, she felt defeated.

"There is definitely an us if you want there to be." At Clay's words, she raised her eyes to meet his directly. He was running one hand through his hair with his head cocked to the side looking at her from under his long lashes.

Swoon.

"I'd like that. I definitely want an us too, but—"

She hated using but. That word negated every one that came before it.

"I mean, yes, there is an us. I decided we're a thing so deal with it." Ronny stunned herself with that last sentence. That was classic old Ronny, so maybe not all of her was gone.

"I appreciate that you're concerned with me and if I'm okay with being touched. I get it, I've told you more details than I have anyone except Jess and my therapists. I also want to tell you everything. The good, the bad, and the ugly. Your perceptiveness and concern are a few of the things that I love about you. I just don't want it to always be you having to think and not live in the moments that we share."

Oh crap, I just dropped the L word, maybe he won't notice if I just keep talking. Bury it in a pile of other words.

"You helped me learn to live in the present at your expense. That's not what I want for you. I'm stronger because of you and I'm braver. I am ready for things I never thought possible, and I promise you right now . . ." She walked into his body and wrapped him in her embrace.

When he returned it, she continued, "I will let you know if and when I'm uncomfortable if you promise to get lost in the moments with me."

Clay kissed her temple while they enjoyed a few moments of closeness. His scent floated around them like a comforting cloud of evergreen, musk, and flannel. If flannel had a scent, it was Clay. When he broke their standing snuggle, it was to cradle her cheeks and stare into her eyes.

The intensity in his grey-blue eyes was knee buckling, but he didn't let her fall. The crooked smirk that she'd come to adore was firmly in place.

"So, you have a list of things you love about me, huh? I think we should discuss some of the other points. How long is it? Do you have it written down so—"

"Oh my god, stop it." Ronny tried to pull away as embarrassment shot through her. *So much for burying it in words hoping he wouldn't notice.*

Clay's answer was to kiss her stupid. It felt normal to be teased like that. And normal for her was better than anything she could have imagined.

Ending the kiss with quick smacking ones, Clay pulled away and dropped his hands to her hips. "Okay, I'll put your list on hold for now. I came by to see if you were up for a trip. I want to show you my place and you can check out the cabinet pulls you picked out and maybe help with some other design points."

"Sure, let me grab my purse." Grabbing her bag took a lot longer than it would for most people. It wasn't by the door with her keys, as a matter of fact, she didn't even have a purse ready.

After snagging one from her closet she threw some things in, including her ID.

"Knock, knock." She startled at Clay's voice right at her bedroom door. When she turned an apology was forthcoming, she could tell, but that's not what she wanted. She forced herself to relax and just wave him in casually.

When he stepped in, he shoved his hands in his jean pockets and gave that shy crooked head look. "I was thinking . . . If you wanted to, you could pack an overnight bag and spend my first night in my house with me. I could cook you dinner, we could watch a movie, and nothing else or everything else. No pressure. Even if you come, still, no pressure."

Ronny couldn't say yes fast enough. When something felt right, it felt right.

CLAYTON

Yes, she said yes.

Clay couldn't believe it. He'd come here to invite her to dinner. He wanted to share his first dinner in his house with her, but after what happened on the porch, he had to take a shot.

He half expected her to say no, that she wasn't ready, and he would have understood. She'd surprised him from the moment they met, even more so today.

The worry that she wasn't strong enough to fit into his life was completely crushed by her words.

The ride to his place was mostly silent. More than once, Ronny broke it to compliment his music tastes. *Something else that makes us a pretty good match.*

It felt natural to joke with her. "Thank god, because if you didn't like Pearl Jam, I could never trust you as a person." He felt her laughter in every chamber of his heart. He was a goner. All the halfway in love with her BS was just him trying to fight it. Because, seriously, who builds a lasting relationship in a couple of weeks? Halfway was a lie, he was all in.

It was not his plan, he'd expected to date for six months, having had sex at least once, then get engaged. After a six to eight-month engagement, then marriage. After two years, start building a family.

But Ronny decimated all his rules. Not just by the type of woman he expected but everything after that too. He'd been clinging to that plan so hard he almost let the person he believed was his soul mate slip away.

When Ronny's hand bumped his thigh, it pulled him from his thoughts. She had her pinkie out and was wiggling it. Dropping one hand from the wheel, he wrapped his pinkie around hers. He took his eyes off the road for a minute and realized she'd scooted closer to him. He liked it.

"So, besides dissing Pearl Jam, what other ways someone can lose your trust?"

"Well, there's not appreciating the masterpiece that is The Dukes of Hazzard."

"Yeah, I gathered that already, what else?" She scooted even closer and dropped her head on his shoulder.

"Lying will do it. I appreciate honesty, even when it hurts. Mom's mac 'n' cheese is a national treasure and I could never ever trust anyone who thinks otherwise. Not returning trust is kind of a big one too. How could I trust someone who didn't trust me?"

The way she stiffened next to him, gave him pause. Maybe he imagined it, maybe it was him projecting. He still harbored guilt over the toilet deception.

"What about you? What are your trust breakers?"

She burrowed a little tighter against him. "The same. I'm different though, I'm afraid if I give my trust and it's betrayed, I don't know if I can ever give it again. I know it's not fair because human beings make mistakes, but in the spirit of honesty . . ." He felt her shrug and his heart sank. Would his deception, the thing that brought them together, be the thing that ripped them apart for good?

Before he could dwell on it for too long, they arrived at his place. He stopped in front of the trailer since it still sat in the front yard.

"Is that your office?" Ronny's attention was behind them.

"Yep. It's an old gas station I converted. Got that and forty-five acres for a great deal. This is where I've been staying while I finished the house. I was going to drag it off and light it on fire, but now I'm thinking of salvaging it. Drag it to the back corner of the property by the lake and maybe rent it out to Charlie or something."

After he shut the truck off, he went around and opened the door for Ronny. She snagged her bag and they took the trail of pavers to the front door of his house.

It just felt right having her here. He knew it was irrational to be that attached to someone he'd only known a short period of time. But the fact was, with every passing moment, every word, every smile, he fell harder and faster.

Ronny standing there, waiting patiently for him to open the door made him smile. It hit him how the universe was working with them.

Mrs. Wilson, Charlie, Jess, Rusty, even her late Gram. All had a hand in bringing them together. He couldn't forget his mom. He'd stop by his parents' house earlier and she'd been weeding the flower beds in the front.

When he'd approached and she'd turned to look up at him, the smile she wore he hadn't seen in a long time.

When she stood and hugged him, neither cared about the potting soil she transferred to his shirt. "What's made my boy so happy? Please tell me it's a who instead of a what?"

And that was why he was here smiling like a weirdo at Ronny. His mom had asked a million questions about her and his expectations. If it weren't for her wisdom, he might not have even brought her here now. Mom had told him time was just an excuse to justify people's fears or explain their failures.

"Use it to your advantage instead. Time has stolen enough from your Ronny, why let it steal more? Rob it instead. Take her fear and your plan and say no more, thumb your nose at old father time and that man who stole from her."

Clay pushed open the door. "Welcome." He bit his tongue on *home*, but it was what he felt in his bones. He was practically walking on air as they entered. However, the sound of a toilet repeatedly flushing in his head kept pulling his feet back to the ground.

"Oh, wow." Ronny dropped her bag as she walked through the open downstairs floor plan. Clay studied her reaction as she took in the wood flooring and sparse furnishings.

He held the door open while Roscoe trotted out and did his business and came back in.

"I haven't had time to pick out new furniture yet. I brought over the couch, a couple of old barstools, and my mattress from the trailer temporarily. But I really want new stuff for the new house. Fresh start, you know?"

After Ronny greeted Roscoe with pets, he headed back to his bed. Trailing her finger along the marble counter she looked completely lost in thought. He'd seen that look before, when she was looking at the design catalog. The lightening of his heart was instantaneous. She was in her element, seeing his . . . hopefully, their house as a blank canvas.

"You did an amazing job with the hardware. I was hoping you might help me pick out furnishings and design elements and whatnot." In a lower voice he added, "Things you'd want in your home."

Luckily, she hadn't heard the last sentence because she was staring at the cabinets with a look that lit up his whole world.

"Wow, they look great. They highlight the simple lines of the cabinetry and make the backsplash pop."

No longer able to resist touching her, Clay wrapped his arms around her from behind, widened his stance, and rested his chin on her shoulder. "What else would you do if this was your place?"

When her arms crossed his and she gently caressed his back and forth, he was practically in heaven. "Well, what I'd do for a bachelor versus a family versus me would all be completely different. Design is more about the person than anything else."

His clarification was immediate. "What would you do for your family, for us." It was a testing of waters. He hadn't exactly said *it,* but he said it.

"First, I'd add pendant lighting over the bar. A basic cylinder design. Either marbled grey, or no, wait, clear glass with Edison bulbs. Then, I'd replace the vent hood with a curved glass one that would complement the lighting. Oh, I have a million ideas."

Kissing her cheek, Clay let her go and pulled out a stool. "Sit here." He retrieved a pen and paper from a kitchen drawer and placed them in front of her.

"You keep talking and write down your ideas while I make you my mom's meatloaf and mac 'n' cheese."

Opening the refrigerator, he pulled out two disposable pans and a bottle of wine. "Well, make is a bit of an overstatement. Wine?" he asked as he set the items on the counter and preheated the oven. Grabbing two glasses, he poured before she answered.

Without looking up from her list, she spoke as if she hadn't heard a word he said after cheese. "Won't that take forever? What do you think of dark gray?"

"I love it and no, thirty minutes tops. I was going to throw together jarred spaghetti sauce and boxed pasta, but Mom insisted on meatloaf."

The pen stopped abruptly and Ronny turned her unique gaze to him. "You told your mom about me?"

Nod.

The pen went flat and she grabbed her stemless glass and took a sip before crossing her arms over her chest. "So, you knew I'd say yes to tonight?"

"No, but I was optimistic. Mom, on the other hand, was thoroughly convinced of her son's persuasion abilities." He clinked his glass to hers sitting on the counter. "But she also wanted to be a part of my first dinner in the new house without intruding. This was the compromise."

She picked up the pen and pointed at him. "You are full of surprises, Mr. Briggs. Now tell me, what do you think of airplanes? More specifically, airplane propellers?"

"Well, I think they are essential to keeping the bird airborne."

Her laugh echoed in the empty space and surrounded him. "You're funny, I mean as a design element. The open space and the size of the living room requires a larger ceiling fan. And anything that large would be a focal point, so I was thinking of a fan that mimics an old plane propeller. What do you think?"

"I think it sounds perfect."

Ronny continued asking questions and making suggestions while the food cooked.

"Oh my god, that is the best-looking meatloaf I've seen since Gram's, which I haven't had since elementary school." Clay served up their plates and sat beside her.

"Well, I hope it's close to what you remember, since Mom used your Gram's recipe."

"Ummm." Her moaning was giving him very dirty thoughts. "Wow, this is amazing. It is just like Gram's. It takes me back." She continued eating and he continued watching her eat. He found everything about her appealing, even the way she swallowed was sexy.

She set her fork down and finished the bite of mac and cheese she'd been eating. "How is it we never met if your mom was close enough to Gram to have her meatloaf recipe? Gram protected that with a shotgun and fairy spells. Wait, who's your mom?"

Clay stopped eating and took a drink of wine. "She said you'd know her as Aunt Meri. And we did actually meet once, I was five. I didn't remember until Mom told me. You were visiting and we had more cucumbers in the garden that year than Mom knew what to do with. She'd already canned enough pickles to feed a small country."

Ronny pushed her plate away and grabbed her wine. She was hanging on his every word. "Well, Mrs. Jackson told her to bring the rest over because she had an idea. Your Gram and my mom, transformed two laundry baskets full of overgrown cucumbers into cinnamon apple rings and you kissed me."

Ronny choked on the wine, so he patted her on the back. "You okay?"

"Oh my god, I remember that."

VERONICA

"**Y**eah?" Clay set his glass down and cupped her cheeks. "Was I that good then, or am I better now?" He lowered his lips to hers torturously slow. Her eyes shuttered closed in anticipation, but his lips didn't touch hers.

When she opened them to see what the holdup was, he was looking right into her eyes. That half smile that brought her to her knees was firmly in place, how had she not recognized that.

She remembered an arrogant little boy who sat on the porch swing and told her she would kiss him that day before he left because it was all part of his plan.

She'd stubbornly folded her arms and refused to kiss him or even look at him. But he just sat there beside her with that same half grin and insisted that she would.

He'd spent hours, so it seemed at the time, talking about his plan. A plan that, according to him, he added her to the minute he saw her. *"My plan is written in stone, so you might as well just get it over with."*

She felt stupid, how could she have forgotten that day. He had irritated her so bad that she actually had kissed him so he would shut up about his plan.

Of course, that *was* his plan and he'd gloated about how his plans always work out. She argued it was a pity kiss and he argued it didn't matter because a kiss was a kiss.

Her lips were tingling just waiting for his kiss. but now, *he* was part of *her* plan, so she grabbed his face and smashed her lips to his.

After the initial contact, she pulled back enough for Clay to take over. She liked the way he kissed her, so she preferred it when he led the dance.

When he pulled back that half grin was gone and he was smiling with his whole face. "Yep, just like when I was five."

Ronny smacked his arm. He'd turned fully on his stool and leaned forward to wrap his arms around her waist. "I knew there was something about you when I saw you in the window that day. It wasn't until Mom was telling me the story that I remembered."

Brushing a lock of hair from his forehead, she put her arms around his neck. "Do you still have your plan? Did you get everything you wanted?"

Clay gave her a hit-and-run kiss and fused their foreheads together. "Yes and no. I got so caught up in my plan that I almost missed out on someone amazing. I almost missed out on you. I had to toss the plan and start listening to my heart."

It was her turn to hit-and-run kiss. "But that's not true." Her hands moved to his face to distance him enough to look into his eyes. "I don't know what you added to your plan since then, but I was part of your plan from age five. That means, I always was, no matter what you did after. I was never informed that I had been removed from it, so, none of that counted."

Watching the emotion play across his facial features and understanding dawn in his eyes loosened her tongue and made her want to leap.

"I know this is fast . . . and I know you may not feel the same way but if the last year of my life has taught me anything, it's taught me to live. *You* taught me to live. Clayton Briggs, I think . . . I mean, I know."

You can do it, just say it. If he doesn't feel the same you can live with that, but you can't live with regrets. Don't let that vile man steal your chance at love.

"I love you. I don't ex—"

His kiss was not metered in the slightest. It was feral and raw. Every ounce of emotion she felt, he seemed to mirror and pour it into her through his lips.

By the time he pulled back, they were both panting. Emotion swirled around them like the eye of a storm. The moment felt significant and pivotal.

"Veronica Beth Allen, I know beyond a shadow of a doubt that I love you. Will you marry me?" They both seemed shocked by the last four words.

"You want to marry me?" She hated that her voice sounded more hopeful than not.

Clay stood and started pacing. *That's not a good sign.* He was dragging his hands through his hair and pacing back and forth, back and forth.

She had to put a stop to this, she couldn't watch his discomfort one second longer. There was no regret on her part for putting her truth out there. But there was regret for spurring him into a proposal he clearly wasn't ready for.

"Look, Clay. I didn't tell you that because I expected anything. I spoke my truth and I don't regret it, but you obviously regret your words." She grabbed his arm. She needed his undivided attention, so he understood.

"I didn't tell you because I wanted anything from you. I told you because I needed to, plain and simple."

"I know that, Ronny. It's not who you are."

"But you obviously said words you didn't mean, and I'm—"

"I didn't say a single syllable I didn't mean."

Color me confused. "Then why do you look like you've been sentenced to hang instead of someone in love?"

Clay stomped to the couch and dropped onto the well-worn surface. Head in hands and looking utterly defeated. Ronny wanted to slink away and never show her face around him again. How could she have gone from so high to so low in two point five seconds? That had to be some sort of record.

"Because that's what it feels like right now. I have something I need to tell you and when I do, you'll walk out that door and take your light with you. Hanging would be a quicker death, but you deserve to know. So, just let me blurt it out and then I'll get you home safe, I promise."

Her heart hit her stomach so hard she almost wretched when it settled there. This was not good, not at all.

Clay wasn't looking at her, he was talking through his hands and everything had gone south so fast. She slunk over to her bag she'd dropped by the door and shouldered it, crossing her arms as she waited for the truth that would shatter her all over again. After three hundred and . . .

Her mind went to count, but the days since her attack didn't have a number anymore. Clay had done that, he took that number and pulverized it, now he was pulverizing her heart.

When he started speaking, she had no trouble hearing him even with the gap in space between them.

The house, or rather the parts she'd seen, was spacious, but the emptiness caused his voice to echo. A sound she'd appreciated when he declared his love but hated now that he would tell her why it was a lie.

"I broke the toilet."

She wasn't sure what she expected him to say, but it wasn't that. What did that have to do with anything anyway?

"Clay?"

He stood and stalked closer to her, stopping just out of arm's reach.

"Don't you see? Our whole relationship started on a lie. I wanted to see you, and with what I thought I knew about you and what I knew about Mom, I thought . . . Well, it doesn't matter. What matters is I lied to you, deceived you, and now I ruined us."

His defeat broke her. The bag slid off her arm and thudded to the floor. It was that sound that kicked her brain into gear and his words finally registered. He broke the toilet so he could see her. He ended up doing so much for her because of that stupid toilet.

Laughter started in her soul, spilled into her heart, and out of her throat. Clay snapped his head to her and looked at her like she'd lost her mind. He was utterly miserable and deserved for it to end but she was giddy.

"Oh my god." She pulled herself together and threw her arms around him. "I didn't know it was possible to love a person more than I did five minutes ago, but I do."

He was still standing there like a statue, not returning her embrace.

"But..."

"If you don't hug me back, I'm going to get a complex."

His physical response was immediate. Wrapped in his arms with his lips at her temple was exactly where she wanted to be.

"Clay, I don't see that as a lie, I mean technically deceptions are lies and I'm very black and white on the issue, but recently I have learned there is a lot of gray in the world and it's not all bad."

The posture of his body relaxed a bit. "I've been torn up about it since the second I did it. Once I spent time with you and watched you put potato chips on your sandwich, I convinced myself it didn't matter. The ends justify the means kind of mentality. But the more I got to know you, the more it ate away at me. In the truck, my heart broke because I thought it was a deal breaker."

His confession eased her own guilt, but all she could focus on was him wanting to spend time with her.

"How could I be upset when you wanted to know me so bad, you'd do something out of character? And what you've given me because of it, I can't even put into words. You changed everything."

He put some distance between their bodies, drawing her attention to his face. "You changed everything, Ronny. You did that, I was just a part of it." The kiss they shared was a slow burn type of kiss but there was no mistaking the underlying tone.

"I guess since we're clearing the air, I need to come clean too. If I held the toilet against you, you'd have to hold the garbage disposal against me."

He looked amused with one eyebrow raised. "Seriously, you did that on purpose. How?"

"I fed it potatoes until it got sick, pretty much the story of my twenty first year of life."

Laughter shook his body. "Well, if we can't forgive each other then Jess is screwed too."

"Wait, you knew about the dryer? When?"

"I could ask you the same thing."

Ronny laughed. "She told me the next day. You?"

"I knew the minute I saw it."

"Wow, what a destructive bunch we are."

It amused her to no end that both her best friend and the man she loved broke things for her.

"Since Jess wanted us together as bad as we wanted to be together, what do you say? Three people tried to destroy a home to bring us together, the least we can do is try to build this new one."

"So, for clarification, you're still proposing?" He held up a finger asking her to wait just a second and disappeared down the hall.

She could hear him rummaging around in something. "Hey, boy." She made her way to the corner of the room and sat on Roscoe's bed next to him.

Clay returned and sat on the other corner of the now crowded dog bed. "I'm supposed to do this on one knee and offer you a ring worth two month's salary. I hate to disappoint you but I'm not on my knees and I don't have an expensive ring yet. What I do have is this fine hound here"—he laid his hand on Roscoe's head— "and this. Veronica Beth Allen, will you marry me?"

With a nod and a barely audible yes, she leaned over the fine hound in question and kissed Clay's chiseled jaw. He took her left hand and slid something on her finger. When she looked down, tears fell from her eyes. "Is that a hose clamp, a really tiny hose clamp?"

"Yeah. I'll get you a real ring. We can go whenever you want to pick it out or I can surprise you."

"This is perfect. Can I just keep it for a while? It means so much more than just a diamond would. This brought us together."

"Back together."

"I'm not sure a pity kiss from a few decades ago counts as our foundation." They stood and he took her in his arms once again.

"Of course, it does. Because you were always part of the plan, even if neither of us knew it."

"Okay, fine, I concede that point."

After a quick kiss, he pulled back with a question in his eyes. "So, what now?" The tiny loop of steel on her finger gave her the extra push she needed to ask for what she wanted.

"I was hoping you would take me upstairs and christen the new place. I want the only memory my body has of a man to be a memory of you."

Clay picked her up like she weighed twenty pounds. "No pressure, right?" There was a slightly nervous note to his voice that told her while he jested with his words, there was a little truth to them.

Once they had safely ascended the steps, she grabbed his face and turned it down to hers. "Never any pressure, but even if there were, I know you're the man for the job. You've helped me repair everything else already, that's all that's left."

CLAYTON

EPILOGUE

8 months later

"**A**re you going to the showroom today?" Clay asked his wife over breakfast. That word still gave him goosebumps. He reached over their plates and fingered the hose clamp she wore on a chain now that she had a proper ring.

It was still Gram and Jess's place in her mind. "No, I think I'll stay home another day. Enjoy the new jetted tub you installed. That thing is magic."

She pulled his hand down to the table and locked her pinkie to his. Of all the small ways they showed their affection, it was his favorite. It was the first touch they shared as adults and it was special.

Pushing her eggs across her plate, she looked like she had something to talk about, but she kept her mouth closed so Clay didn't push her.

After placing his plate in the sink, he kissed her on the forehead and grabbed his toolbelt. "I'll be back within the hour, just a quick trip to Mrs. Wilson's for some minor goat issue or another. Probably the mean old one busting through the fence again."

That wasn't the issue at all, and he knew it, but it wasn't technically a lie. And it wasn't to deceive her, it was to hold off knowledge for an hour or so. That's all.

"Well, I'll be here. Give Mrs. Wilson my love. Oh, and call your mom, she has something she needs you for this weekend.

"Will do." He kissed her goodbye one last time and headed out. The old trailer was moved to the back forty for Charlie so he could see her standing in the door all the way to the road.

It was their morning routine and he loved it. Most mornings though, she was dressed to be the design guru she was. She'd followed through with her and her Gram's plan to turn her house into a design showroom. Jess still lived there and ran the business equally with Ronny.

The girls had more clients than they knew what to do with. Bellwood had needed some style for too long. He was worried about her lately. She'd shunned work for the last week. At first he'd been concerned she was slipping back to a bad place, but she assured him she wasn't and so had his mom.

It was still hard to see her not enjoying life the way she had been. But he had a feeling Daisy Duke was going to change all that. He used his Bluetooth to call his mom on the way over to Mrs. Wilson's.

"Hello, son."

"Hey, Mom. How are you?"

"Perfect, and how are you and Ronny?"

Yeah, she never just asked about him anymore, which was nice.

"Good all around. So, what do you need this weekend?"

"I wanted to surprise Ronny with a celebration of Sophia. Monday would have been her eightieth birthday and I want to celebrate how everything has come full circle, you know?"

"Yeah, I know. I think that's great Mom, and Ronny will love it so much she'll cry. What do you need me to do for it?"

"Nothing, just have her here at one on Saturday, but don't tell her what we're doing." Clay had pulled up at Mrs. Wilson's and switched the conversation to his phone.

"Will do. I gotta run, Mom, I'm picking up Daisy today. Is there anything else you need?"

"Grandbabies, lots of grandbabies. Love you, son."

"I'll do my best. Love you, Mom."

Clay shook his head as he headed toward the barn where he could see Mrs. Wilson. His mom started asking for grandbabies before he'd even invited Ronny to dinner that night. He couldn't wait for her to be carrying his child either.

It was all part of his new and improved plan. It hadn't happened for them yet, but they would have Roscoe and Daisy to raise until it did.

"Hi, Mrs. Wilson."

"Oh, hello, Clayton. How's Ronny?"

"She's good. She'll be even better after she meets Daisy there. Is she ready to go?"

"Yep, but can you lean that piece of wood against that tiny hole over there first?" Puzzled he did as he was bid. "There, now you repaired my barn. So, no lies involved since I am sure you told her that to slip away."

The old lady was sharp. "Actually, I think I used the phrase, 'minor goat issue with the fence or something.' But thank you, you're the best."

Mrs. Wilson picked up the snow-white goat and handed her over to Clay. "She's more than ready. She's a screamer that one. Hope you're ready for that. Hey," she said and slapped him on the arm as they walked toward his truck, "it'll be good practice for all the grandbabies you'll be having for Meredith. Huh?"

She elbowed him and waggled her eyebrows; the old woman was incorrigible. He opened the door and put a harness on Daisy and hooked her to the seatbelt, just in case.

Turning to Mrs. Wilson, he said with humor, "I'm trying every chance I get." The old lady laughed and gave him a nod of approval before heading inside.

Clay drove off singing Pearl Jam songs to his new girl. He used voice to text to tease Ronny. Thank goodness for farm roads, zero traffic.

> CLAY: I just repaired old lady Wilson's goat barn and thought of you.
> RONNY: Wow, goats make you think of me? How did you stay single for so long with that level of game?

> CLAY: Smartass. Goats are adorable and so are you, but that's not why. I thought Roscoe P. Coltrane could use a friend, and you could use a goat named Daisy Duke.

> RONNY: She sounds lovely, and Roscoe could use the distraction in about 7 months.

> CLAY: What's happening in 7 months?

> RONNY: He'll have a new job as protector.

> CLAY: Of what? Gravy Train farts?

> RONNY: OMG, no. LOL

A string of emojis followed but didn't display on his truck radio screen.

> CLAY: ???

> RONNY: I'm pregnant, you big dummy. I didn't want to tell you in a text but I'm the worst at keeping secrets. Are you mad I didn't do some elaborate way to tell you?

> RONNY: Clay? Say something, please?

> CLAY: Look outside. The happiest man in the world just pulled up. He'll be wearing a huge smile and holding a baby goat.

> CLAY: I love you more than life itself.

> RONNY: Ditto.

> RONNY: See you in 3 seconds.

> CLAY: Make it 2.

> RONNY: I'll shoot for 1.

When she came rushing out the door with Roscoe hot on her heels, she looked different than just an hour ago, because Clay was seeing her through a different lens.

Perfection.

She was perfect. They were perfect and their growing family was better than perfect. "Oh my god, look at her. Gimme." She lifted little Daisy from his arms and buried her face in her neck. "She's so beautiful."

"You're beautiful." Clay couldn't resist rubbing her belly. His future, everything he ever wanted was right here within arm's reach.

"Are you happy?"

"More than you can ever know. I love you so much, Ronny. You took my plan, wadded it up, and tossed it in the trash, but you gave me a future. One that is far superior to my plan."

Her contented sigh settled in his bones and they walked back inside as a family that had a different shape, but a family all the same.

"I love you, Clayton Briggs, but if you so much as utter the name Luke, Bo, or Duke as possible baby names, I am taking Daisy and Roscoe and moving into the trailer with Charlie."

"Well, there's always Uncle Jessie. It works for either a boy or a girl. Not to mention Jess will love us even more because she'll think we named the baby after her, so free sitter." Ronny rolled her eyes and settled on the couch with the dog and the goat leaving no room for him.

"Nope. Not going to happen."

"Well, you might want to revisit Bo or Luke because what's left is Boss Hogg and Cooter and I do not think you want to go there."

She was laughing again, and so was he. Roscoe was howling, and Daisy was screaming, it was chaos. But the kind that made it feel like *home.* "Oh my god, stop already. We are not naming our child after your favorite TV show. Even they agree with me."

Clay scooted Roscoe over and settled in with his arm around Ronny's shoulders. She stroked Daisy, and Roscoe weaseled his way onto his lap.

"Well, if the Dukes are out, would you consider our favorite band? Eddie has a nice ring to it?"

Daisy screamed, Roscoe howled, and they laughed.

Yep, one happy family.

THE END

DEAR READER

I hope you enjoyed your first #LoveHack story.

More hacks are coming.

Each #LoveHack tale will be a completely stand-alone read, connected only by the theme of hacking it. While Clay and Ronny's tale was a contemporary and clean romance, not all will be. Coming #LoveHack stories will be different tropes and heat levels.

Did you fall in love with Clay & Ronny? Please, consider leaving a review so other readers can hack it too.

Verlene

PLAYLIST

This is the playlist the characters in this book "shared" with me as theirs. I listened to this music while writing the book to connect with them.

"Broken" (a song by Seether feat. Amy Lee)
"Let Love In" (a song by The Goo Goo Dolls)
"Pieces" (a song by Rob Thomas)
"Closer to You" (a song by The Wallflowers)
"Black" (a song by Pearl Jam)
"Big Empty" (a song by Stone Temple Pilots)
"Down in a Hole" (a song by Alice In Chains)
"Black Hole Sun" (a song by Soundgarden)
"Heart-Shaped Box" (a song by Nirvana)
"Breath" (a song by Breaking Benjamin)
"Under Your Scars" (a song by Godsmack)
"Blackbird" (a song by Sarah Darling)
"Scars to Your Beautiful" (a song by Alessia Cara)
"You Saved Me from Myself" (a song by Colin Hay)

NO endorsement by the artists or their representatives is given or implied by sharing this list. I hold no rights to any music/song listed here.

Listen on Spotify. http://smarturl.it/DIYHeartsPlaylist

ACKNOWLEDGMENTS

First and foremost, as always, I must give my family a nod. Thanks for keeping your expectations low so I can meet them while trying to get books out. I love you more than I thought I was capable of.

Missy, thanks for not totally giving up on me when I am weeks late with getting my manuscript to you. I half expect you to tell me to go fuck myself, and to date, you haven't said that to my face, so winning.

Sam, thanks for letting me reference your books and name. But more than that, thanks for getting me when I don't get myself half the damn time. You've been a better friend than I deserve.

Vixens and BAR Team, I adore each and every one of you. I forget to send prizes, or post daily, and go LIVE when I promised, but y'all forgive me and keep posting hot guys and funny memes. Y'all make me smile.

Amber, I don't know if you know it, but banana Nicolas Cage showed up at a particularly difficult part in this book. It helped more than you know. I never thought I'd be grateful for something like that, but here I am saying thanks.

If I didn't mention you and you helped me out in any way during this book, thanks. If I didn't mention you and you didn't help, then that's why, so . . .

Verlene

BOOKS BY VERLENE

ANTHOLOGIES

Vegas Strong
(Charity: The Code Green Campaign)
Bad to the Bone: a bad boy anthology

CONNECTED NOVELLAS
(connected stand-alone reads)

Room 15
The Last Resort Motel
Be Supportive
Escaping the Friend Zone

ORDERED SERIES
(best read in order)

IMAGINE INK
Indelible You *Imagine Ink 1*
Brand Me *Imagine Ink 2*
Irrevocably Mine *Imagine Ink 3*
Inevitably Yours *Imagine Ink 4*
Unmistakably Us *Imagine Ink 5*

STAND-ALONE

Ryder Hard
DIY Hearts
#LoveHack

ABOUT VERLENE

Verlene was born and raised in the south. Thanks to the military, she's traveled the US, but now calls Sin City home. Self-proclaimed zombie apocalypse enthusiast, word porn peddler, human canvas, Manowarrior, serial grammar killer, rabid Bama fan, accidental dust bunny population specialist, and abuser of the word f*ck. She's thrown live grenades, survived the tear gas chamber and forced road marches, but still thinks writing and publishing are more brutal.

She's written countless stories and poems but didn't start publishing until 2015.

Verlene is on a mission to make naughty the new normal, one book at a time.

Scan below for ways to connect with Verlene.

If you want to stay up to date on my latest releases & happenings...

- Subscribe to my newsletter
  www.verlenelandon.com/signmeup
- Follow me on Amazon & Bookbub
  search VERLENE LANDON on both or
  smarturl.it/VLAmazon
  smarturl.it/VerleneBookBub

If you like a healthy dose of naughty fun, giveaways, and sneak peeks at upcoming books before anyone else, join my Facebook reader group, Verlene's Vixens

- facebook.com/groups/VerleneLandon

I love to connect with readers, so feel free to use any of my links to find me online.

- Facebook Page: Author Verlene Landon
- Facebook Profile: Verlene Landon
- Instagram: Verlene.Landon
- Twitter: Verlene_Landon
- Signed Books & Merchandise: VerleneLandon.com/store
- Email: Verlene@VerleneLandon.com or Verlene.Landon@gmail.com